Whilst the names used are those of real people, the story, the context in which those names are used, the characterisations, and the incidents portrayed in this production are dramatisations, and therefore should not be treated as factual. This fictional approach to the identification of actual persons (living or deceased), places, buildings, and products is intended; therefore, no historical facts should be inferred.

E-Book ISBN 978-1-0686686-2-3
Print ISBN 978-1-0686686-3-0

Book Cover and illustrations by the author

First Edition 2025

Through His Eyes

By

Bruce A J McLauchlan

INDEX

IN THE BEGINNING

It was a strange transition. I left my Father's side (willingly, aware of that which must transpire) to become but one single cell, housed in a warm and comforting place. I could feel the added warmth that came from the sun that we had created; the slight dip in temperature outside that place as the sun descended below the horizon; the almost imperceptible pull on my mother's waters inside that place as our moon rose to pass across the sky in pursuit of that setting sun. That pull was just a little stronger as our moon waxed, and oh so tiny a dip as it waned, on its perpetual cycle.

As the days passed, one cell became two, became four, became eight, became sixteen; slowly I grew. I drew on my mother's energy resources to feed my rapidly growing human body; so too, I drew on her emotional outputs. Her doubts infused me: why had she been chosen; was she worthy; would she be able to raise me, her firstborn, in a due and proper way. There were also her natural fears: of the pain of childbirth; of providing for me. I felt her love enfolding me too. I absorbed that love; it gave strength to that which would be the human part of me.

As my body took shape, I started to learn movement anew; I stretched, I turned. I felt my mother's hands pressed to her belly; I felt her joy when she experienced my first kick (delivered just for her!). And then there was a larger pair of hands, my father's, that I rewarded with another push from my leg. I felt his joy too, mingled with wonder and awe; it made it all real for him now. Suddenly, the realisation struck: he was going to be a father!

Outside of that place, my Heavenly Father scanned the firmament, searching for a star to watch over me; perhaps his thoughts were something akin to yours when you buy a mobile to place above the cot of a newborn. Maybe that is where you got the idea from? He found the perfect star, named it Joy, and set it on a trajectory to be at its brightest when it was above the place where I would stay after I was born.

Joseph and Mary – I must get used to calling them Mum and Dad – did not notice the star. But others did.

In distant lands, astronomers and magi saw the star's approach; they knew that it was significant, though they knew not why. They met at night to discuss its possible meanings; by now, they had noted its slow, ponderous progress across the sky, moving as other stars did not. It was this movement that informed their decision to follow it. Thirty set out, some astride camels, others keeping pace on foot. It would be a long and wearisome journey, but not one of them ever considered turning back. To them, the star was wonderful. It drew them on; its pull magnetic, almost gravitational in its urgency. Three led the party from the front; you will record their names as Gaspar,

Balthasar, and Melchior. And who am I to contradict you!

Not long after they had set out, and when they were still very distant, a messenger arrived with instructions for all citizens to return to their place of origin: a census was to be taken. The journey would be hard on my mother; her belly was swollen as I grew larger within it each day. My father did not have anywhere near enough to buy a donkey; he did, however, find a landowner prepared to loan him one in exchange for the promise of several large wooden tools (ploughs, yokes, and the like) when we returned. And so we set out on what might be counted as my first journey. I knew that I would make many more journeys in the future, but this one was important: Rome had, unbeknownst to them, set me on a trajectory that ensured that my birth would happen in the place prophesied. My Father uses all to his ends!

The Roman authorities showed no concern that the upheaval of this census came during our Feast of Tabernacles. Many grumbled about the timing, which was ironic really, as the festival remembers the time when we were nomads and wandering in the wilderness, sleeping rough! But such was the feeling towards Rome at the time that anything that they did was criticised; sometimes reasonably, sometimes irrationally.

Whilst I had no window to watch the progress of our journey, my spirit showed me clearly everything that we passed by. Some of our travels crossed arable lands, where friendly shepherds and farmers called out greetings; they must have lived there all of their lives, as they had not set out to travel to any other place. At other times the going was harsh, with just sand and rocks along our path; these called no friendly greetings. The rhythmic amble of the donkey was soothing to both my mother and me. Mary slept on occasion, with my earthly father's hand, solid, strong, with a craftsman's callouses, holding her in place. I slept too. Well, it was a kind of sleep; that is the best way to describe it at least; I slept for much of the time.

When we had travelled as far as we could each day, we slept by the side of the track that we were following. It was cold at night: Mum and Dad (slowly, I was getting used to calling them that) huddled together, next to the donkey, each giving warmth to the other. As we drew nearer to our destination, Bethlehem, we joined others along the way; it became a merrier time. Often at night there would be singing and the sharing of food.

BIRTH

The sun was just starting to descend, to scrape the horizon, as we arrived in Bethlehem. The town was in chaos! So many people had arrived, all within such a short period of time that the town's infrastructure was straining to cope with it. Everyone wanted to be fed; everyone wanted to drink something; nearly everyone was looking for a place to sleep – many days on the road made even the hardiest long for a proper bed! Mum knew that her time was near. She gripped Dad's arm. "Joseph, we must find a place to offer shelter! I cannot give birth in the town square!" I felt alarm suffuse Dad; he had given scant thought to this, being too absorbed in the journey itself. "Wait here," he said. "I will find what I can, though my hopes are low."

He hurried off, pleading our case wherever he could; he started with communal taverns, and then, receiving the same reply time after time, he started trying private dwellings. Most were sympathetic to his predicament, they really wanted to help, but every space was full. Now he was close to the very edge of town; the properties were thinning out; the hustle and bustle was less. Dad knocked on the door of a small, low, stone building, repeating his plea when a stooped old man came to the door. The old man sighed resignedly. "I am sorry, my friend; I have but this one room, which has barely enough space for me." "Thank you, anyway." Dad turned to go.

"Wait, it is in a very sorry state of repairs, but I do have yonder stable. It will not be too clean; I hardly go in it now that I can no longer work." Dad looked across and saw a low wooden building; there were holes in the roof and some of the walls; the door hung on one hinge; there was loose straw everywhere. It wasn't what he wanted, but he knew it was the best he would get. "How much for a few nights?" "My friend, I could not make a charge for so poor a dwelling. Return it to me cleaner than it was and I will be happy."

Somewhat sheepishly, Dad described the place that he had found to Mum. I felt her heart sink, but she tried not to show it; she knew that he had done his best. "Well, lead on," she said with a smile. "I am certain that we can make it comfortable."

Mum found a brush from somewhere and set busily about sweeping out much of the dust. The stable was not big: three stalls and an open area in front of those. None of the straw was fresh, but Mum sorted out several piles of the better stems, bundling them into one of the stalls for her and Dad to sleep on. In another, she made a bed for our donkey and tied a sheaf to the doorpost for him to graze upon. Whilst she was doing that, Dad had managed to repair the second hinge, so now the door hung properly and could be drawn closed. There was not much that he could immediately do about the holes in the roof, but he did patch those in the days ahead. We only had the one small lamp, but it cast just enough light for them to see to their tasks as the sun was now well and truly set. At just a few minutes to midnight, they settled down on the straw to sleep; Mum's head was resting on Dad's shoulder, his protective arm around her. They were both exhausted, from the journey and from the work; within seconds, they were both sleeping.

Around four hours later, Mum gently woke Dad up. "It is my time," she said. I half expected him to panic, but he was calm, methodical, practical as he set about helping Mum as best he could. There was no midwife to call upon.

As I came into the world, I felt my mother's pain. I empathised, but I could not help it. She cried out. I did what I could (which was not much) to see that the birth would be as quick as it could be. As Mum lay back to draw breath, Dad cut my cord and settled me onto Mum. Dad lay down beside us; for a long while the three of us just lay there; their arms were lightly around each other, and I was between them. Whilst Mum fed me, Dad filled the manger that was on the side of our stall with straw. I was wrapped tightly, now, in cloths. My hunger sated, Mum placed me gently in the manger to sleep. Despite the slightly scratchy straw, I shed no tears. Awareness has its advantages: no fears that I would not be fed, no lack of understanding, no fear of strangers (there were of course no strangers: I knew them all; knew them better than they knew themselves!).

Whilst I was aware, just like all newborns, I still had to learn to control my muscles, my coordination, and how to operate my vocal cords, so don't expect me to start spouting wise words – or any words – just yet.

It was the same later when I began to learn my dad's trade. Let me tell you, there were a few early pieces that I made which did end up straight on the bonfire! Maybe I learned more quickly than some, or perhaps my dad was just an excellent teacher! But more of that, later.

As I lay there on that first morning, I received my first visitors. It was only appropriate that that visit came from shepherds! My Father had sent his messengers out into the surrounding fields, where they declared my arrival to the shepherds as they sat tending their flocks (as I would tend mine in the future). I guess, in a strange way, he was as excited as any new father, and wanted to shout about the birth of his son to everyone who would listen! At first, they had cowered in fear, but soon they were filled with wonder, both at the message and that they were the first to hear it! They were but lowly shepherds; sheep herding and fishing were not considered dream jobs! That wonder had now driven them to the stable where I rested; they brought with them a newborn lamb, which they presented to my dad. He felt very bad that he had naught more than a few pieces of flatbread to share with them, but they did not seem to notice as they stared in awe at my newly awoken form in that manger.

I had another "visitor" that morning, one who would visit each and every day. Looking out through the gap in the wall, made by the crude frame that bordered the window opening, I cannot tell you of the sheer joy that I experienced when I saw the sunrise through human eyes; of course, I knew that it was a thing of beauty, but to see it with human eyes truly brought its majesty home. That first morning I watched as variegated rays of sunlight prised their way, finger-like, through the gaps in the roof and the walls. I watched the tiny motes of dust, stirred up from the dry earth floor, as they danced in those rays, expressing their own joy, their welcome, for the new day. It would be the same in the future: the first time that I saw the waves gently lapping at the seashore, and so too when I saw the majestic mountains sweeping up to awe-inspiring heights. They were a source of wonder and amazement; these, too, I knew before, but I'm not sure I truly knew them until I saw them with human eyes. I guess there are many other things that I could add to that list of wonders: the rain; my first full moon; rainbows; morning dew on my toes; even the sounds of nature greeting the dawn.

There is a downside to being aware, though: I knew the day of my circumcision was approaching; it was to come on the eighth day after my birth. And whilst the pain of that would be nothing compared to that which I would suffer in the future, it was still not something I was looking forward to. This was, after all, the first time that I would experience physical pain! Sure, I'd felt emotional pain, spiritual sadness, and even empathised with human suffering, but this was to be a first for me.

It did hurt! And it also gave me some insight to the pain that lay ahead of me that had now become a reality. Outside my human body, I had known only mental anguish, never physical pain. Physical pain was new to me. Emotional pain I had experienced many times before, especially each time one of you went astray. But I was ignorant of physical pain. Somewhat foolishly, perhaps even with a shade of arrogance, I had imagined physical and emotional pain being very similar. And in some ways they are, as, of course, many of you will know. Which is the most painful? Who can say. For each of us it will differ; of course, the cause at the root of each is a significant determining factor. The death of a loved one hurts more than a stubbed toe; but then a spear wound hurts more than being treated with scorn. Most of the time, anyway!

We were still living in that stable; Dad was doing some odd jobs for our host and a couple of other families around Bethlehem too. He had virtually no money left and so was saving up for what he thought would be a return journey – he did not yet know that we were going to take an entirely different route! On my fortieth day, Mum and Dad took me on the short two- or three-league journey to the Temple in Jerusalem for my dedication; I was, after all, their firstborn. We entered the Temple at the same time as an old man; he was white of hair, long of beard, with wrinkled, weathered skin. His eyes were rheumy and dim of sight; those eyes misted over more when he saw me with tears in his eyes, and yet he saw more clearly than he had for years. This was Simeon, and this is what he said when he saw me in Mum's arms: "Oh! Blessed day! It was foretold that I would see this one before my day of passing, and yet I did not quite believe it. Old I am now, I have forgotten how many years it has been since my birth, but I know that my last days will soon be here." He reached out a hesitant hand to touch my brow. "That I should be blessed to see the Messiah before that last day!" The tears fell from those opaque eyes; Mum put me into his arms (she was already getting used to the idea that she was going to have to share me!). He looked at me closely; he saw me clearly, though he could see very little else. "And now I have held him too, my life has reached completion. Bless the three of you, but especially bless the child for what he will become." After a while he passed me back to Mum and walked slowly from the Temple, deep in reverie. That night he passed and now awaits my return like so many others. Not much further along, we met Anna. Anna had been living in the Temple now for many years, since the passing of her husband, who she had been married to for only seven years (they had been seven very happy years). Now she devoted her life to my Father, working on the upkeep of the Temple, praying and fasting. Father had blessed her with the gift of prophesy. She too fussed over me and recognised me for who I am: "Happy, blessed, day! That I should live to see the Messiah brought here; that I should have the chance to hold him!" Her eighty-four years fell from her; she was like a teenager again, positively skipping! She bustled off, "Oh, oh, oh, I must tell everyone! I must share this wonderful news! Who should I tell first?" She reeled off a whole list of names, marking them off on her fingers. She, too, would soon pass from this world, but for the remainder of her days she had a permanent smile upon her face; she beamed; she radiated positivity; she told everyone that she met about me.

Sadly, the rabbi who oversaw my dedication had no such foresight. His ministrations were perfunctory, routine, the words simply delivered by rote. I was just one of a long line of infants who would be brought before him; he saw none of them for who they were. The appropriate words having been spoken, we returned to our stable in Bethlehem. As we returned, Mum and Dad spoke about the dedication; they agreed that the rabbi really did not seem to care in any way about me or any of the other babes that he saw. That made Mum sad. But the time with Simeon, and with Anna, gave her great joy. She thought deeply on these things.

And then, four days later, the astronomers and wise men arrived. They brought gifts (three in particular you will be familiar with); they brought praises; they brought many questions, most of which Mum and Dad could only answer in part – or not at all!

They told us that Herod himself wanted to come and pay homage. Dad was incredulous – most of the things that had happened over the last ten months or so had left him feeling so! The visitors themselves were clearly very sceptical: not that he wanted to visit, but concerning the true purpose of that visit.

MY EXODUS TO EGYPT

Frustrated in his plans, with the wise men and astronomers returning home by an unexpected route, Herod was filled with rage. His barbaric, atavistic wrath caused him to yell out his edict that all newborns and those up to two years in age should be slaughtered. The ripples of that pronouncement echoed throughout the land; so much horror was to follow. He was not the first to make such a proclamation; he had clearly learned nothing from those who had instigated it in the past!

I heard it loud and clear; Mum and Dad heard it only as distant echoes of a rumour and of gossip. But it did not matter: Dad, having been warned in dreams of this by my Father, had already set off for Egypt with Mum and me.

To be truthful, I remember little of my time in Egypt, no, no, it's not an age thing; it's more of a blurring of all the exodus and redemption tales that have happened and how they have been told; one fact blurring with another. I suppose you might say that our exodus was self-imposed, whereas others were enforced; I'd describe that as a moot point!

Our exile was different in many ways; there was no triumphal escape. We lived quietly, day by day; Dad earning (sometimes money, but more often than not simply meals) by plying his trade.

Eventually, word reached us that Herod was dead, and we felt able to return home. Four hundred days had passed since our arrival in Egypt; I was one year and two months (440 days) old. We had spent one day there for every year that the Israelites had spent under Pharoh, before Moses led them to freedom. As we returned, having arranged passage with a caravan of folk who were also making that same return journey, Dad started fretting over his debt to the owner of the donkey who had taken us to Bethlehem. We had returned the donkey on our way down to Egypt, but our quick exit had not allowed any time for Dad to keep his side of the bargain. Would the landowner be angry? Would he have Dad thrown into debtors jail? Worse? Whilst I was not yet talking of course, I'm not sure that the words of an infant would have prevented my Dad from such fretting anyway.

SIGHT

Very early on, I learned to separate that which I saw with my human eyes and that which I saw with my… … … how can I describe it? Deeper vision? Take my first rabbi. Now, I "knew" that he was fifty-three years and two months (and nine days) old; however, my five-year-old human eyes saw him as "incredibly old". So that is how I knew I must see him; I compartmentalised. It was the same with the games I played with the other kids: I suppose that I could have won them all. But to do so would not have been human: you cannot win all the time at everything. So it had to be with me.

Sure, there were myriad occasions throughout my life when I had to be superhuman, especially when drawing on my deeper knowledge, but I just knew it could not, should not, be all the time.

It is virtually impossible to put into words my state of being both wholly aware (through my Spirit's Eye) and wholly unaware through my human composition. Just as I had had to develop and train my muscles, my coordination, my skills, so too was it with my mind, brain and thinking – if I write I knew everything and nothing at the same time, it would be factual and yet tell you nothing at all. I was both wholly human and wholly divine; those two were robustly, immovably connected and yet also disconnected, separate, incompatible – like trying to push together the north poles of two magnets. Lying on a couch in the twenty-first century, I might have been described as possessing dissociative identity disorder, yet that was not it at all either. Picture me on two sides of a chasm at the same time – a chasm with no bottom – a rickety woven-vine-and-wood bridge spans the two sides; the vine ropes are frayed, and the wooden slats are rotting and missing in places. Occasionally I can cross over, when the need to (and the courage to) drives me; but at other times such connection is quite beyond me. On another day, that bridge might be a work of precision engineering, solid, sturdy, easily traversed; so too are there times when the gap narrows and I can just step across. Is that a helpful way of picturing it? As I grew, both my human abilities and my divine abilities grew too; they went from latent to potent.

Both needed to develop; both needed courage and leaps of faith at times. So, there may be times when you are thinking to yourself, but surely, Jesus would have known that – hopefully this describes well to you why I might not! This description feels important to seek to convey; I hope that it might help you understand those occasions when you are thinking – doubting – well, he must have known this, so why did he do that? We can all be wise after an event!

Could I not close the metaphorical gap between the human and the divine? Sure. Sometimes it was indeed closed – and not by my doing. But the gap was vital to who I was; the tension was entirely necessary. I had to be both. Except for one moment in time; I'll come back to that later, towards the end of this story.

THE TRINITY AND THE SPIRIT

It seems that at this point I should try to explain too – if I can – the relationship of the Trinity in connection with my birth; the relationship of Father, Son and Holy Spirit; how we are both one and separate at the same time. Much easier said than done! I brought the Father's love (that knows no bounds) to the world, and for the world, through grace (that passes all understanding) to you. The Holy Spirit is the rope that binds the three of us together, and binds all of you to us (in strength) through fellowship.

Maybe a start point is to picture a prism and the effect that it has on light, which is both one colour and seven (or more) colours at the same time. But that is not really it. Maybe consider that fundamental of life – water – that can be ice and liquid and steam; but try to picture it being all three of those at the same time. Closer but still not really right, as those are three separate states, and I know you will not be able to help but picture the heat, or lack of it, associated with those states, where we are one and the same together. Let me think about it a bit more, maybe I'll come up with a better explanation later.

Actually, let's have one other stab. Think about it as that love that I referred to. The spirit is, in a way, another manifestation of our love for you; a conduit for grace. You'll have felt love, particularly if you have known love towards your children. It's something like that – a lot, actually, as we do love you as our children – a bonded love. You know how you cannot "see" love? And yet you can, when you see that couple together, and just a glance shows you how much love there is between them. There is another aspect: the Spirit is both a manifestation our love for you, and the breath of life itself. All living things have – need – both. Plants and trees need to breathe, just as we do. It is also true to say that the wind itself is the breath of life, taking the seeds and scattering them for the plants, so they have no need of a farmer to tend them.

I keep using the word love, it is the closest that I can get in your tongue. The Greeks, of course, had many different words for love, which is a little more helpful; these included eros (ἔρως), for physical/sexual love; philia (φιλία), for affection; agape (ἀγάπη) as a sacrificial love, such as saving a child whom you have never met from the jaws of a lion; storgé (στοργή), love of family, of children; mania (μανία) describing that which might, politely, be called obsessive love; lūdus (ερωτοτροπία), for courting or, perhaps, flirting; pragma (πράγμα), for a strategic agreement, say, between the son of one king and the daughter of another, or one family and another; philautia (φιλαυτία), the love of self. From that list, storgé is probably the closest, and philia, although those in themselves do not go quite far enough. Does all that help in any way?

MY APPRENTICESHIP

It turned out that the deal Dad had struck around the loan of that donkey on which we travelled to Bethlehem brought us unforeseen benefits. True to his word, Dad paid back the landowner (who completely forgave him what might have been seen as late payment, when he saw the quantity and quality of the repayment) with a goodly selection of tools and implements; as was Dad's way, he did not seek to cut corners or use cheaper elements in their creation – he took his usual pride in their creation. So impressed was the landowner, that, after the debt was paid, a new deal was reached for my earthly father to become a regular supplier and to be paid for his services. These wages he stored up alongside the gold that had been gifted to me at my birth; eventually, this allowed Dad to build and equip a workshop and establish himself as a craftsman of note. Orders started to come in from others too, meaning that his days were long and arduous; but he faced the challenge with joy and with a smile on his face.

Mention of the gold might prompt you to ask what had happened to the resins of frankincense and myrrh that had also been gifted to us. Mum eked those out over many years: some we would burn as incense on special days; some to remove odours on the hotter summer days; the very last smattering of tiny pieces were combined with nard and other resins and were there with me in my tomb.

From my ninth birthday, I started to help out in the workshop. At first doing nothing more than sweeping up and tidying away the tools that were used by Dad and the three others who now worked with him. How I loved the smell of sawdust, which pervaded everything. It is one of my earliest earthly memories, that aroma of freshly cut wood announcing Dad's return from work; the smell never left him – and I say that in the most positive of ways!

After a year or so of sweeping and tidying, I was trusted to undertake some carpentry. Of course, just simple hand tools to begin with. And let me tell you, I made a right mess of making these in the beginning – most of my early efforts ended up as firewood. As I mentioned right back at the start of my tale, my body was that of a human, with all its strengths and frailties; I still needed to train my muscles to undertake new tasks; there were no instant, overnight, successes!

The time came for my next lesson, an advancement from the creation of simple tools. I'd carved and shaped; I'd whittled and smoothed; now Dad set me the task of making my first joint. "This will not be to scale," he said, "but I want you to imagine that you are creating the shaft for the front of a wagon. A hand cart, or one pulled by oxen; the principle is the same: a main shaft and then a cross piece. You have seen me make many, so let's see how you get on."

He handed me two pieces of wood: one around a cubit and a half long, one just under a cubit; both were around a seventh of a cubit wide and the same deep. I was fully determined to make him proud of my work, so took the greatest of care. On the longer piece, I sawed two grooves, closer to one end, sawing each as close as I could make it to halfway through. And then, with hammer and chisel, I cut away the wood in between those two saw cuts. This was the trickier stage. I took great care, chipping away only small amounts at a time. With a sandstone block, I smoothed away some of the roughness against the grain of the wood. Then, taking the shorter spar, I repeated what I had just done, but this time, the two saw cuts were at the centre. Once this was chiselled and smooth, the ultimate test came: fitting the two pieces together. I laid the longer spar on the bench, and then placed the other on top of it, so that my two chiselled gaps aligned; then, with the mallet, I tapped the top one down so that the two pieces meshed together. My cutting had been good, as the top piece sank into the bottom; the two pieces aligned so that neither stood proud, nor did one sink lower. The joint was tight; of course, it would need to be bound to make it fully robust (at least, it would if it was to be a working joint, not just a training exercise).

I was so happy with my work! I picked it up to show Dad, beaming. But then I saw the shape that I held before me. The cross! As suddenly as it had come, my smile withered, and under a tsunami of emotions, mixing complex human hormonal changes (I was, after all, on the cusp of becoming a teenager!) with those of my future awareness, I began to tremble. A tear came to my eye.

Mistaking my emotions for something else, Dad put his hand on my shoulder. “My son! Do not be ashamed; this is wonderful workmanship! It far surpasses my first effort when I made it, although that was many years ago now.” My trembling grew worse, and I could not answer him. He drew me close, into his embrace, until my trembling and crying ceased.

At that moment, a customer entered the shop, so Dad wasn’t able to ask me why I wept (besides, he thought that he knew). We were so busy for the rest of the day that I had no chance to tell him; although how I would have told him, what I would have told him, I cannot say. Perhaps it was not something that at that age I could have put into meaningful words. After all, many years later when I started talking to my disciples about the cross, even they didn’t understand until afterwards, did they?

IN THE TEMPLE

The second big change in my life occurred at the Temple. Whilst I had been attending the Temple for some while now, my part was only to sit silently and listen. I was only too willing to do that! To hear how you read from those great and insightful scrolls; how you pored over, and discovered sometimes the connections that we had helped you to create, linking the content of one scroll with that of another.

Even then, some saw the threat that they perceived in me; they sought to test me. On perhaps the fifth or sixth time I was asked to read from the Scriptures, I was handed the scroll concerning what you now call Genesis 3. I had finished the reading and decided to supplement the reading with a little bit of extra teaching. It was the first time that I had tried this, and it taught me a valuable lesson on how my lessons would be perceived in the future also; the rabbi saw my words as overweening arrogance, of ideas far and above both my age and my station in life!

I had said: "It was in that moment of encouraged mistrust, that Adam and Eve sought wisdom for which they were not yet ready. They saw wisdom as a valuable thing; it felt to them that to know good from evil could only be helpful. They had not considered that knowing evil might, through temptation, drive them to commit evil itself. They had lived in a blissful innocence up until that point, now they had the weight of discernment upon their shoulders; they knew evil for what it was, but that also meant that they could – and indeed would – face the dilemma of doing something bad if they thought the good of the outcome might outweigh the evil of the deed. But they were unable to see outcomes in the same way that YHWH could." I knew that it was not yet the time to start referring to Him as *my Father*. One step at a time. "And so YHWH had no choice but to deliver of his word and cast them from the Garden. They must commit their carnage outside that place, until they had gained sufficient of the wisdom that they had craved so badly to cease to do evil, and be allowed to re-enter the Garden."

The rabbi sought to tie me in a knot, to cause me to stumble; whilst there were only a few people in the synagogue, he had no wish for a mere child to seem more insightful than he, so he asked me a question that he thought that I would be unable to answer: "Tell me then," he said, "are you saying that YHWH lied when He said that to eat of the tree of the knowledge of good and evil death would be the result?" I answered with a question of my own: "Are you saying to me that you will live forever?" He had no answer other than anger! Grabbing a broom from one of those who were busily cleaning the synagogue, he chased me out of the Temple and down the street in a most unseemly manner! "And don't come back!" he yelled, the broom held high like a spear as I turned a final corner and ducked out of sight. Of course, I did return but that particular rabbi studiously avoided me thereafter.

THE DEATH OF JOSEPH: FROM DAD'S BUSINESS TO MY FATHER'S BUSINESS

In my twenty-third year, pain and tragedy fell upon me like a rock. I had been working all day in the workshop with Dad; it was a hot and humid day, and we were both sweating from the heat and the effort applied to our task: we were assembling all the component parts of a cart that we had been building for the previous month or so. Several of those pieces, such as the wheels and axles, were weighty with their inherent requirement to be robust; it took the two of us to lift them using ropes and pulleys too so that we could lift and assemble everything. Looking back, I can see now that Dad was sweating more than he might usually have done. As we moved through to our private dwellings behind the workshop, he stumbled and fell. In moments my mum was at his side; together, we lifted him onto his pallet. Mum brought water and a cloth, mopping down his fevered brow. We both stayed with him into the evening, any thoughts of an evening meal far from our minds.

I sat there holding my father's hand as the life slipped away from him; the tears streaming down my cheeks, dripping unabated into my lap. Dad was surrounded, too, by my brothers and sisters; we all wept; we all knew these were his last hours. He knew it too; he had passed his blessing and the workshop on to me. But I knew that soon I would pass that on to James to hold: this was a clear sign that I must soon come into my ministry. But first there needed to be a long period of reflection and meditation and, of course, prayerful conversations with my Father. Much longer than the forty days I would later spend in the wilderness.

Often I wondered if, had I come into my own earlier, I could have called him back. But then I knew only that the times of healing were ahead of me; I did not know that on occasion I would raise the dead (only my Heavenly Father knows all things). The inheritance meant little to me. All things must be passed on; they are ours to hold but for a short while.

For a while, I was wholly human in my grief.

Now my mum and my siblings looked to me to be the breadwinner for the family. I had learned all that Dad could teach me; he had taught my brothers, somewhat, too; now, in turn, I started to teach those remaining skills to my brothers: to James, Joses, Simon and little Jude. James was only just over a year younger than me and soon became as adept as I – perhaps even more so – at the skills of carpentry; he had already had some training from our dad too. Jude was too small at that point to use any of the tools of our trade; but he would enthusiastically sweep up the sawdust and avidly watch as we fulfilled the orders that we had taken for those in the village: implements for farming, for the home (and indeed to construct homes), and for several other trades besides.

As we developed the business, each of us took on a specialism, as that helped us to sell our skills to customers. The business grew and became even more successful; but I knew that soon I must leave it behind and set about my real purpose in the world. I was reluctant to start the journey, in part as I knew where and how it would end, but I was also really enjoying my time living with my loving family around me. It was a busy life; at times it was hard, but always it was filled with love. I perhaps put it off longer than I should have.

When the summer came to an end and trade dwindled as the end of the year approached, I knew it was time for me to leave; a clear and compelling dream came to me – one which it was impossible to ignore. By now, James, Joses, Simon, and Jude, were all working fully effectively in our carpentry business. James and Joses were fully competent carpenters; Simon was also close to the end of his apprenticeship; little Jude still did not do much more than sweeping and tidying at the moment, as he was still very young. Mum also had my sister Mary and her younger sister Salome to help her. They would miss me, but the business and the home did not need me there to function. It was time for me to wander from synagogue to synagogue to learn. It was not the Scriptures themselves that I needed to learn (I had been studying them for many years and, of course, in one way had had a hand in their writing!); I wanted to observe the priests undertaking their teachings, and, equally importantly, those who came to listen. Desert communities I visited also, experiencing and sharing in their hardships. For brief periods, I dwelled alone in the hills and mountains, where I would pray and reflect on the things that I was learning.

COUSIN JOHN

It was around the same time that I left our carpentry business behind that Cousin John also set off to begin his ministry; I was not to see him again for a good few years. It felt like a double loss: my family and my friend; both were painful, as he had always been my earthly confidante, the first one who truly knew me after my parents.

I will never forget my first meeting with my cousin, all those years ago. Whilst he was not, actually, that much older than me, he of course looked so much older in my child's eyes. Even then he was like a great big ball of fuzz! His hair, wiry, unruly, unkempt; usually straw and twigs lay buried within it – testament to the trees that he would climb; he would always get so much higher than anyone else dared to go, partly as he did not seem to mind (or even notice) the scratches he got from the sharper growths. In fact, I often teased him about finding birds nesting in his hair, or would rummage around and tell him I was looking for eggs!

The human in me looked up to him, and he treated me as his kid brother. Sometimes he was rough with me, besting me in wrestling matches every time (except one, when I got lucky), but woe betide anyone else who might pick on me; he would defend me with a ferocity that reminded me of rough seas pounding on rocks.

We grew up together, although we were also often apart, as he would disappear (much to the chagrin of his mother, who would fret until she grew used to the fact that John was very much his own master with a unique path to travel), only to return many days later even more unkempt – and unwashed! There were many rumours concerning that which John did in these times: that he went into the wilderness to wrestle wild animals (including lions); that he went deeper into the desert than any man had gone before; that he descended into caves to commune with beings that no other man has seen; that he climbed to the highest peaks to be closer to God and on occasion speak directly with Him; some even claimed that he travelled to other worlds!

Of course I knew the whole truth, even though there was a certain veracity in all of the rumours, but that was not for me to share then, and is not for me to share now. John's tale is his to tell!

THE TIME FOR A RETURN

As I sat one evening around a glowing fire, chatting to those with whom I had been travelling for some while now, a newcomer arrived. He brought many tales, one of which really made me sit up and take notice: "But now, let me tell you about this fellow who I came across one day whilst travelling along the banks of the Jordan. Huge he was, ruddy and hairy. And how bristly that hair was: matted and wiry; long about his shoulders. His clothing was of coarse camel hair, cinched at the waist with a leather band!

"He was stood in the river water roaring out to people that they should join him in the water, that they should allow him to baptise them in those waters, to wash away their past misdemeanours, to prepare for the arrival of someone he said was soon to come. I'm not sure who it was of whom he spoke, but he sounded to be a wonderous individual; perhaps even the promised Messiah?

"It was strange, too, that although he shouted at the crowds, railed against them, gave them short shrift, still they seemed to flock to him. On one occasion he even cursed some of the Pharisees who had come to witness what all the fuss was about: 'you brood of vipers!' he called out! Can you imagine that? To abuse such authorities as those!"

Yes, I could imagine that. I knew without a shadow of doubt who he was referring to; I imagine that you have guessed it too?

For a long while he sat there, telling us more tales of John, telling us also of others whom he had met, of places that he had visited. Those tales were how he paid for the supper that we shared with him. Eventually, as his tales came to an end, we settled down to sleep. Although, I could not sleep. For a long while I lay there, wrapped in my cloak but staring, eyes wide, at the dwindling flames and the glowing red embers that followed them. As the glow of the fire subsided, the intricate blanket of stars sharpened. Embers and stars. Stars and embers. Together they told me what I already knew: John's ministry was intensified; mine must too. I prayed to my Father, asking him how I should begin. His answer was clear: *whilst you have no sin to wash away, a baptism also symbolises a new start. Seek out John*.

MY BAPTISM

Two days since, I had left the caravan; now I was drawing near to the banks of the Jordan. I had not hurried; many thoughts had occupied my mind as I walked. As I drew near to the river's bank, I mused: how many have missed the repetitions, the overlaps, the links between the old writings and the new writings that were to come after my time. Indeed, many characters might be said to have appeared and then reappeared. Perhaps the best example is that of my friend and cousin John, who was in many ways also Elijah, although also not him – despite what many said.

John was easy enough to find; I simply needed to follow the stream of people and the general hubbub. Whilst there was no queue as such, neither was there jostling nor pushing or shoving. We approached as one. John saw me and motioned for me to step forward, but I waved his request away; I would await my turn. Above us, not a single wisp of cloud blotted the deep azure of the sky; occasionally a black speck would race across it: a small bird in search of corn or an insect. As I drew nearer, the waters imparted their usual sonic influence upon the sounds: the clamour of the crowd grew less, the voices out in the water became magnified. I heard John's deep, sonorous, tones (the perfect match for his appearance!): "Do you renounce all sin?"

"I do."

"Will you follow only the one true God, cleaving only to Him?"

"I will."

"Will you leave the past behind you and tread only the new path?"

"I will."

"Do you give your whole to God to use as he will?"

"I do."

"Then, I baptise you in the new hope, in the name of the one who is to come" (he glanced across at me) "in the certainty of eternal life in his kingdom!"

This liturgy was followed by the soft sounds of water splashing as John dipped them backwards, below the surface. Some emerged silently, deep in their thoughts; some emerged loudly, voicing the joy and their praises; some cried out a single word; some had a flow of tears, mixing with the waters as they ran from their skin and hair.

Mostly it was men who approached John, but there were a few women amongst them, further increasing the anger of those who proclaimed themselves priests and holy authorities, who stood watching from further up the bank. They shook their heads, and occasionally their fists, as they whispered together in both vocal and tacit intrigue, declaring those in the water apostatic and worse. They were still looking for *him* to occupy that empty seat at the Passover banquet table, clothed in splendour, not to be coarsely dressed in the muddy waters of the Jordan; they did not see who he truly was. Now it was my turn to enter the water; I left my sandals by the shore and waded out. The soft mud of the riverbed squidged between my toes; the waters themselves were at a temperature that felt neither cool nor warm against my skin; a light breeze puffed across the waters; a single white cloud scudded into the sky, as though wanting to watch that which was about to transpire.

As I drew nearer to John, many emotions passed across his face, amongst them humility, revelation, fear, wonder, awe, belief (but also disbelief that I had come to him), and a few other emotions that I struggled to put a name to. At first we embraced, two long-lost friends. I looked deeply into his eyes. "It is time to wash off the past and set my feet upon the appointed path." His humility took precedence: "But Lord, I am not worthy to wash even your feet!" I held his gaze, putting a reassuring hand upon his shoulder. "And yet, it must be so. You are the gate that opens onto that path." He bowed his head in acquiescence, murmuring "Let it be so."

As John dipped my body backwards, immersing me in the water, wholly, I heard my Father's voice; he told me, “My son, all that you have achieved so far you have achieved with my hand on your shoulder. Now the full measure of the Spirit shall join you, too, so the baptism you now participate in is not to wash away previous sins and misdemeanours – you have none. It is so that you are rebirthed and that you may be truly mantled in our Spirit.” And then a wondrous thing happened as John drew me back out of the water: the heavens broke open, right where that cloud had been, and, like a blaze of lights, a dove (although larger) came descending towards me; he was as white and bright as the moon on those dark and cloudless nights. Then, as he drew near to me, suddenly, he blazed golden, as bright and golden as the sun. He settled upon me, his wings enfolded me, and then, like ice melting on a hot rock, he seemed to sink beneath my flesh, and I truly was born anew. Words rumbled across the valley like tumbling boulders: “This is my beloved Son; he is my delight; in him I am well pleased!”

IN THE WILDERNESS

With the waters of the Jordan still damp on my clothes, I headed south and into the wilderness. How I would long for that moisture in the days to come! I had left quickly and quietly to ensure that none sought to come with me – although, in truth, I had not yet gathered any sort of real following; I had come to the river alone, leaving friends (and family) behind.

Sand clung to my feet, rubbing against my sandals; in places it tore my skin. It was the first of many pains that I would suffer in the coming days. I pulled a fold from my robe further over my head, shielding my eyes from the glare of the scorching sun. I had only my staff. No water skin. But then no skin would have held enough for the time ahead of me.

The wilderness is an inhospitable place. And that is exactly why I sought it out. The distractions would be fewer and by their very nature, therefore, deeper. They all revolved around the fundamentals of life: eating, drinking, sleeping. Yes, sleeping was hard; when a cold hunger gnaws at your stomach and a deep thirst grips at your throat (גרון), sleep is not easy. Stony pillows and sand everywhere are not a help either, but those were minor and soon forgotten.

For the first few days, I managed little, other than trying to suppress the calls of my body. But, slowly, I found an inner strength, a place of balance; I was able to begin my meditations. I spoke daily with my

Father on all that was ahead of me. Internal debate I held too: how? when? what? where?

Many wild animals gathered around me; they meant me no harm; perhaps they gained solidarity from our both suffering from a lack of food and of moisture, together. There was an impasse between the larger animals and me: neither would seek to subdue and eat the other; with the smaller animals, on an instinctual level they knew that they were not destined to become my food. The angels attended me, too, sustained me. At first, I had sent them away, thinking they were a crutch that I did not need; worse, that it was somewhat sidestepping this challenge. But then I realised that it was just my Father's way of being with me as he is with all of us as we face trials and tribulations. Guiding and supporting, not taking over. They did not sustain me with food, or with drink; no, nourishment came through that which they brought me from my Father: meditations, encouragements, wisdom. The angels did not take away my thirst or my hunger – that was essential for my spiritual journey – but they kept me from death. Sometimes, they would bring word from my Father; on other occasions, I would speak with him directly. It became my habit to start each day with the same prayer; it was one I was to repeat throughout my life. Slowly, over the years, I would refine the wording, but this is how it started:

Father, Father; Abba, Abba!
Glory to your name!

I long for the Day of Your Coming;
When we walk this world together.
Father, help me to do as you would!

Sustain me, sustain me;
Forgive me when things go awry!
Shield me from all temptations,
Make me resolute, night and day.
And, please, keep the evil one at bay.

Shield me, shield me,
Keep me from harm!
Guide me, guide me,
Make my path straight!

For all this is your kingdom;
All power comes from you!
To you, I give all glory!

Amen

MIDDLE DAYS

And now there is another thing that I understand more fully: what it means to be an exile. You may not feel like an exile if you have called the same country home for all your life or even if you have moved from one country to another. I realise that there are still those who are exiled from their homelands by a cruel regime, by a cruel climate (somewhat of your own making – although generally not of the inhabitants' making), or by some disaster (natural or otherwise) or other. But you are all exiles from my Father's Garden. When he and she, who are mother and father to you all, were cast out from the Garden, your exile began; now, that specific memory may be lost, but all of you will recognise that hole, that which it has left behind: a sense of longing. It is the root of the wanderlust that exists for many, or the search for that perfect job, in some, the search for the perfect partner, maybe just a move from one house to another. It is that longing for belonging, for which there is no resolution but that which follows the end days. I, too, was an exile back then: from my Father's House, separated from Heaven, which is my home.

As I had wandered from synagogue to synagogue, and town to town in recent years, now I wandered from rocky outcrop to rocky outcrop. The world had turned beige and grey; there were no other colours to see. Even the occasional piece of stubborn flora that I came across reflected those hues: gnarled, twisted, brown of leaf. By night, I shivered; by day, I sweated – although it was a dry sweat, my body obdurately trying to hold on to the last vestiges of the water that it held.

In my times of sleeping, since the wilderness had become my home of the moment, I had had many dreams. Last night, I had dreamed of a sword. A mighty blade. But I had not dreamed of it as a weapon of death; I had dreamed of its making. Now, as I wandered towards a distant outcrop, that dream came back to me. I started to make sense of its importance (as all dreams are of importance if we remember them rightly). In the desert heat, I too was being forged: forged into a sword of the Spirit. It would be my only piece of armour. And my sword was not to bring death; my sword was to bring life. My sword was to cut through the chains of the Torah that shackled men to mistaken truths; my sword was to cut through the divisions that separated one man from another; my sword was to cut off the branches of the vine that gave bad fruit or no fruit at all.

THE END OF THE FORTY

Those last few days were the hardest. I was famished and dehydrated; small drops of morning dew had been my only sustenance throughout. And of course, it was when I was at my lowest that he came to tempt me. You know who I mean; don't make me name him.

The tempter came in dragon form; he sidled closer, breathing his fire over my toes, my feet. His flames could cause me pain, immense pain, but they could not destroy my flesh.

He came again: shapeless, without form. He takes his shape from the fears of man, often snakes and serpents; but I know him for who he is, so he could not cloud my eyes.

Once, we had been friends. Mighty had he been, great amongst those in my Father's House. But then he let in a small chink; I think it was a jealousy, but I cannot be certain. I saw him less and less; my guess is that he avoided me, as he knew I would see into his heart. But then came the day when his schemes and his desires were revealed to my Father; he and those that he had subjugated were cast out and fell from my Father's House. They were cast down, to land upon the earth.

Our hope for him is like our hope for you – even the wickedest or the most foolish – that, before the end, he and you will repent of your sins and return to us.

If I am honest, I have little hope for him now, but the end has not yet come; it has started, but its full coming is not yet here. But I have jumped near to the end of my story; my story was only just beginning, so let us return to that!

I had been resting in the partial shade of some rocks; a sharp protrusion from one was digging into my back, but I had not the energy to move. It was only in the chill of night when I found some strength to wander in those last days. The time for my return was near, but I feared that I would lack the strength to do so. And now here he was before me, his words not coming from any lips but sown directly into my mind. He turned my eye to a smooth round rock, around a third of a cubit in length. He made me see it crust over as a freshly baked loaf, a shimmer of haze over it showing the residue of heat from the oven; he sent its smell to my nostrils (I would have salivated, but my mouth was too dry). The thought came: *You need but say the word and this will be so*. I found myself of a mind to make it so; after all, it would give me the strength I needed for the return journey. It would be fine, I thought. I started to reach my hand towards it, but then I

heard his voice once more, *yes, yes, do it*, and it gave him away. I knew that whilst the bread would feed my weakened body, it would have the completely opposite effect on my heart and soul. Aloud I cried out, "The Son of Man cannot thrive by bread alone! I live for the words of my Father! They are my food!" Those words echoed in my mind, casting him forth. But he did not leave me; his shapeless form gave the impression of crouching, hunched, frog-like (although larger), some little way off. He brooded. He plotted his next move. And I was too weak to cast him fully away.

The blazing red sun had just passed its zenith, turning, as it seemed, the dusty ground to crimson molten rock. My eyes were drawn through the shimmering of the heat to a distant outcropping, its shape somehow familiar. My eyes followed its lines and its curves seeking an answer. And then I had it! It was the first temple, standing resplendent, cool, welcoming: an oasis in the wilderness. And with that recognition, suddenly I found myself standing on the pinnacle of its tallest tower. I was standing in something of a crenelation, looking down on the temple's magnificence. Cherubim, angels and seraphim encircled the tower; they gathered in other places too. That voice came to me again: *See how they fly below you with open arms; they are primed to catch you should you fall! Why not reward their faith? Step forward; give them the joy of uplifting you! Choose one to save the Saviour. For surely they will do so.* The voice continued to petition, to rattle inside my mind; its words seemed wise. And yet they felt ...

they felt ... false! Realisation came and with it the strength to deny: “It is not for me to put the Lord, my Father, my God, to the test!”

The scene dissolved before me, the falsehoods washed away. But now I was in a place that was even higher; I saw not only Jerusalem, Samaria, and Egypt, but the lands far beyond them too, even unto the milky white expanses that capped and cupped the world. *All this could be yours! Together we could rule all, bringing order where there is chaos, bringing an end to conflict, becoming mighty, but of course, benevolent rulers. The world would bow down before us. All this, I may grant. I ask only, in exchange, that you acknowledge and worship me, that you bow to me as the world will bow to you.* Again, at first the words seemed wise; man did indeed need a firm hand to rule them, too easily were they distracted, led astray, and into sin. Surely, the price was not too much to pay to bring such harmony? But then I looked closer at this world and saw the clouds under which men lived, clouds of fear, oppression, a new kind of slavery, one where all men were slaves. “We do not need such false rule! Long ago it was written: Worship the Lord your God and serve only him!”

Alongside temptation, other wiles did he try, also. He tried to cow me with fear. Many beasts he created to assault me, but I turned them aside. And then a great beast he summoned, one quite different from the others and so terrifying. It had devoured and crushed its other victims with iron teeth and bronze claws, trampling their remains beneath its feet; I saw the detritus that it left in its wake. This beast came towards me; saliva and blood dripped from its jaws, a red tongue hung from its mouth, and many horns adorned its head. Slowly, with stealth, it circled the spot where I sat. I mastered myself as its path went behind me, showing no fear, not turning to look. Thrice he circled me, and then he stopped in front of me. A great roar came from his jaws! Still, I did not quail. He crouched, ready to pounce; still I sat resolute. “Begone foul beast! This is not your place or your time!” A wind arose and blew him away like smoke until nought remained of iron or bronze, flesh or bone. And then I rested.

Thrice he had tempted me. With food. With power. And with all the kingdoms of the world. Four mighty beasts he had brought against me. Temptation upon temptation: the temptation to sin, the temptation to submit to my inner fears, the temptation to resign myself to death (I was indeed resigned to my death, but the ordained one, not this one, for all that it would have been quicker and with less pain). My human body could know such temptations, but my inner self must not be tempted so; it must remain clean.

And so it was that I turned my back on temptations. They would not be the last of my temptations – I knew that more lay before me – and on this, the forty-first day, I returned to the towns and cities of Israel.

THE CHOOSING OF THE DISCIPLES

The first requirement after my return was that of selecting companions. Man is designed for companionship: to live and to work in community. There is a time to be alone – as I had just been, for forty days and for forty nights – but that time is not *all* the time. We designed you, deliberately, in this way. You need friends, you need family, you need society as a whole. I also had another need – I needed those who I knew would be able to continue the mission after my end: to think it, to speak it, to share it, to write it. In some ways their journeys would be harder than mine; for all that I would tell them what lay ahead, I knew that they would not grasp it fully.

Perhaps it was a reaction to those latest events, to choose the very antitheses of those recent days, but I was drawn towards waters: to seas and to lakes. Several I passed in quick succession but knew that they were not the ones; inexorably, I was drawn towards the Sea of Galilee. I arrived just as the long arms of the sun were reaching across the waters to pull back the dark nighttime blankets and reveal the lighter blue sheets beneath. A gentle breeze plucked at the caps of the occasional temperate waves puffing white froth into the air. The fishing boats which had been out all night were just beginning to return to the shore. It had not been a good night for most of them: the boats stood out high and proud above the waters; the gunwales were not scudding along only just above the surface of the water: the catch – if any – had been minimal; no weight dragged them low to the surface.

As I had made my journey to this place, I had – as I had before my sojourn in the wilderness – stopped at temples and other places of gathering to read from the scrolls, to speak, to reason with others. And so, like the waves that now lapped at my toes, words concerning me had spread. Many had heard tales of the young man who spoke with the same authority as the elders, who sometimes even called them to account.

The boats were now all starting to beach themselves along the shore in their regular spots. A short way along from where I stood one with two occupants came ashore; one of these was called Andrew, who had heard my name; the other was called Simon, and he had not heard my name – he was much more interested in the drinking of wine and the playing of games of strength to test his mettle! Further along from them, upwind, another boat was disembarking; one of them shouted with excitement when he saw me, "There he is! It's Jesus! The one that I told you about. I heard him speak the other day when I travelled to the market!" He started to head towards me.

Those words reached Andrew's ears; he grabbed at Simon's sleeve, trying to drag him towards me too. Simon was reluctant: he wanted the numbing comfort of a tavern, not rambling chat from some itinerant prophet! But Andrew was insistent. Soon a couple of dozen fishermen were arrayed before me. I sat down on a tuft of rough grass that doggedly sought to grow up amongst the inhospitable sands. They settled down before me; looking on, expectantly. "Has the catch been good this night?" I began. Heads shook from side to side. "Sometimes, it must be so. Or sometimes the catch will be unexpected. Today, I think, I have caught treasures, though I have cast no nets." My eye settled upon Simon. "This catch I will not be throwing back, although one of the fish thinks he is small and of no significance." We spoke until mid-morning. Then suddenly, I turned again towards Andrew and Simon: "Andrew." He started when I spoke his name, surprised, as he had not introduced himself. "And you, whose name I do not know, or whose name is not right," – I saw his shoulders slump; how could I know Andrew's name but not his – "we must set out to sea again; your catch awaits." Andrew did not answer but neither did he get to his feet. Not so with Simon, he roared out in his internal pain, "Are you crazy? All night we have cast our nets, and yet not one single sprat did we catch! I am weary for my bed."

"Nevertheless, you must trust me, and we must do so." This was his test, and he passed. Although he spoke no words, he headed back towards his boat. Something inside him was stirring. Silently he pushed the boat out into the shallows. Andrew helped me to board, and so the three of us set out. Another boat followed behind in our wake, curious as to what might transpire. Some way out, they made to stop. "No," I said, "we must go deeper." Unquestioningly, they rowed out further until I said, "Here. Now lower your nets." They did so, expecting to catch no more than seaweed – in their eyes, I had not chosen a good spot. But almost no sooner were the nets set out than the small buoys and floats that marked their locations started to bob and dip. There was a catch. And from the movement of those buoys and floats, it was a big one! Simon and Andrew sought to drag the nets towards the boat, but the catch was too large. Just then, the other boat that had been tailing us drew near; it was Zebedee's boat, and with him were his two sons, James and John. "Come help us!" cried Simon across the water. Between them, they lashed the nets securely between the two boats and then unfurled the sails; the sails were instantly filled with a wind which blew them back towards the shore.

As the two boats sailed across the water, their prows high and skipping over the waves, their sterns low, almost parallel with the surface of the sea, as the nets dragged them down, Simon prostrated himself at my feet. No mean feat in a fast-moving and not overly large boat! "Lord, I am a wicked and sinful man. I have done many wrongs; I have violated many of the Torah's laws. But, if you can see beyond those things, then I will follow you wherever you lead." "I do see beyond them. And yes, I think you should follow me; I accept your offer, gladly. Andrew, you too must come with us."

Simon jumped to his feet, partly for joy and partly as we were fast approaching the shoreline. He let the sail drop, as did Zebedee, and then he had leaped over the side into the shallows, further slowing the boat. Several of the other fishermen had remained on the beach side, washing and repairing their nets. Andrew called out to them, "Come! Help us to bring this catch ashore. There is plenty for all!" They did not need to be asked twice: their hauls had all been as bad as each other, and they could see the drag of these nets and, so, how full they must be. It took the two dozen of them to drag the catch ashore; quickly, they sorted them into barrels, loading the larger specimens straight onto their wagons.

Simon snatched up the largest fish from the catch and leaped up onto a rock. The mid-morning rays of the sun, still not at its zenith, caught the scales of the fish and it flared brightly, as though Simon held a torch or beacon aloft. The rays fell on him too, illuminating his face and turning his hair and beard to burnished copper. Holding the fish aloft he roared in a triumphant voice, "Mighty is my Lord Jesus! Great wonders can he perform!" I knew then his true name. "You are Peter, the rock! And as you stand upon that rock, so shall you be the rock upon which my kingdom will be built!" I felt a nudge towards the occupants of the other boat. "James, John, you too should follow. Together, we will fish for men to join us!" At a silent nod from their father, they left him with the two boats. Some of the others resumed their net-mending, whilst the other half came along with the five of us to sell the catch in the market.

I chose the twelve for many reasons, but chief amongst these was that their traits were representative of all. Whilst all those of you who populate this world, then and now, are unique and special, treasured and loved, there are many things that you also share. I don't mean physical traits (although those were represented too) but the somewhat internal traits. You will know yours; you don't need me to tell you what they are, who you are. You will all lean towards one of the twelve who share your traits. You can probably guess many of those represented by the twelve. With Thomas, it was doubt (a trait that seems to grow daily amongst you);

with Peter, anger; with Judas, a taste for the finer things; with Matthew, his methodical, considered approach. I am sure that you recognise others, and from those, the traits that you share.

I was very intentional in the number of disciples that I chose; there would be twelve. In the past, we had chosen twelve glorious, mighty families, of the one mighty family, to lead by example and be the twelve tribes of the chosen race. But they fell many times. And so now I chose twelve rag-tag individuals who, in appearance, were the total opposite of those twelve families but who, in heart, were mightier than all of them.

Let me tell you a bit more about them.

THE CHARACTERS OF THE TWELVE

As I said, I needed to be very intentional in the choosing of my closest friends, my disciples. Originally, I had thought to go with seven (or two lots of seven), but as I spoke with my Father in prayer, it became clear that twelve would be the perfect number as I began to make my choices. Of course, I didn't want twelve identical folks; they needed to be different and disparate in their makeup. My purpose was to make one kingdom from many, and therefore variety was key. And so I chose Matthew (or Levi as he was known when first I met him): bookish, methodical, precise, light-skinned, shy; Peter: originally Simon, my rock, stormy as the seas, hairy, unkempt; John: wise, insightful, considered, resolute; James: brother of John (I called them the Sons of Thunder for their passion and fervour), much the darker skinned of the two, the first of them to die; Andrew: (who had followed Cousin John, before; he was always the seeker) enthusiastic, sturdy, short, but he who travelled the furthest subsequently (as he had before); Philip: keen, enthusiastic, effervescent; Barty: righteous, pious, disciplined, well groomed, shy; Thomas: a real mix in a single frame, resolute, brave, and yet plagued by doubts; James: enigmatic, quiet (but when he spoke, so insightful), diminutive; Thaddeus: inquisitive, discreet, almost as hairy as Peter; Simon: ferocious, wiry, almost as rock-like as Peter, although much fleeter of foot, previously he had been a Zealot; poor Judas: handsome, somewhat vain but also misguided, driven by an inner demon who finally mastered him, yet without whom my story – and therefore yours – would have had a very different ending!

Not one of them had had a formal education; they

were rough, some uncultured, some who could not write (although several of them started to learn over the years, begging Matthew to teach them, which he did, although at first reluctantly, not thinking himself patient enough be a teacher), but with exactly the hearts that I needed. Simon was by far the tallest, James (John's brother) was closest to him in height, but the other James was the smallest of the twelve. You wouldn't call any of them (except Judas) handsome; rugged would be a polite word for the others, although I can think of many other words which would be more accurate! But they were my brothers, and I loved them all. They became family – closer than family – and friends; they were essential to that which followed. In fact, without them, there would have been no follow-on at all!

If you were putting together a team, would you choose as I did? Or would you choose only the best, those whom you knew would rub along well together? In my team, I had those viewed as traitors, as betrayers (although not until the end was this known), as xenophobes; there were fiercely political activists, they rubbed shoulders with nay-sayers and firebrands!

I remember well the first time I saw Matthew – he was totally absorbed within himself. Sure, he spoke to people, with his job he had to. But the real Matthew himself was locked up deep inside. "Come out, Matthew," I commanded. I did not mean from his tax booth, I meant from himself. He looked at me with startled, blinking eyes, like a fawn discovered in the bush; his mouth opened and then closed again. Twice. I saw the light return to his eyes, and then he did leave his booth, careless of the money within. The Roman soldiers nearby would see that it didn't get mislaid, of course. He came to my side, still startled by my summons, not yet able to speak – but I heard him loud enough. He hardly ever left my side again until the time of parting.

In many ways, Simon-Peter and Matthew were the perfect complement to each other. They were the complete opposite of each other! Where Matthew was considered, Simon-Peter was impulsive; where Matthew weighed the pros and cons before acting, Simon would just do it. The other Simon and Barty were also opposites (as were others amongst them): in the Zealot, there was aggression, fight, but in dear sweet, peace-loving Bartholomew: flight. I'm sure that you do not need me to label the others, that you can see their traits for yourself? But, I'm curious, which one do you identify most closely with?

Within fourteen days, I had accumulated the twelve. "Come," I said, "it is time for you to begin your journey with the Son of Man." It was the first time that they had heard that phrase (in fact, it was the first time that I had used it), but it would not be the last.

THE SON OF MAN

Why do I call myself the Son of Man? That is both easy and complex to answer. In part it is to fit with the prophesies and *one coming as a son of man*, but that makes it sound as though I was trying to create something that was not – it was very definitely something that was. In part it was because we made you – man – in our image; and, whilst I was there before you, I came also after you when I was born to Mary. If you came before that, it casts you as father, for I was born to you. So, you could say that I and you alike were all sons of the Adam (אָדָם). There is a third reason – but that is even harder to explain than the first two! We had made you in our image, and here I was clothed in your image.

Oh, and whilst we are on these topics, just one further thought: when it is recorded in books and on scrolls, you often write the word of God. Which is certainly one way of putting it. But those of you who have at some point truly heard the word of God will know that that is not quite how it is. It isn't written. You see it, and yet it isn't truly a vision either. It's simply something that creates a clarity in your mind. You just know it. So perhaps using the phrase a knowing of God might be more accurate? Although also confusing as those words don't quite work when written down!

REVELATION

As it is with you, so it is with me; when my Father made me flesh, he gave me the same free will that he gifted to you. It meant that I could be tempted, diverted, in the same way that you can; it also meant that I had decisions of my own to make – even though I could also ask my Father's guidance (as can you). One of those decisions was the time to start to reveal myself, to start on my true mission. Whilst much of my life – especially the end of it – was preordained, still there were many opportunities for free choice.

And, if I am honest, another thing held me back: that human frailty of doubt. It was indeed a strange mix going on inside my head; I had both unwavering certainty but, at the same time, vestiges of doubt. You cannot live in a human body without having human frailties and human emotions – many of you (most of you!) will know what I mean; you will have that conflict between certainty and doubt, holding that internal debate. So it was with me at that moment. I knew beyond doubt that I had the power, and yet I still had doubt. Doubt about the timing: was it now? Doubt about the task: could I do it? Doubt about the outcome: would the result be received as I wanted? would the underlying message be heard?

Now, I did not think that it was yet the time for that revelation, but circumstances had other ideas! When two of you marry, we delight in that moment; relationship, marriage, was one of our greatest gifts to you. That moment, when two become one, brings us such joy; that relationship is a small reflection of our overall relationship with you.

And here we all were: me, the twelve, my mum, my brothers and sisters, alongside a few other friends; we were all gathered for a wedding celebration. The groom's family were not wealthy; his father ran a small pottery business next to our family's carpentry workshop, so their house was quite crowded, and we spilled out onto the surrounding spaces. But it was a joyous occasion; there was dancing, and we all drank of the red wine that they provided. Some of the guests drank a *lot* of the wine! More than had been allowed for, so it started to run short. They had those who were waiting upon us put less in the goblets, but that just meant that there were demands to fill them more often. There were not sufficient quantities of wine within the village for them to buy more – and even if there had been, they would not have been able to, as the groom's father had spent everything that he had.

I was dimly aware of all of this, but if I am honest, I did not focus much on it; I was enjoying just being a part of the celebrations. I saw the groom's mother talking to my mother, who then moved through the throng towards me. Resting a hand on my forearm, she looked steadily up into my eyes. "My son, they are all but out of wine, I think that you need to help them." Deliberately, I responded as though I had not grasped the import of her words: "But we have no quantities of wine in the house to help them?" "You know that that is not what I meant; but, you know that you can help them if you will!" She did not need to add *I have heard your Heavenly Father prompting me to prompt you*. Often He had communicated to me indirectly through Mum, perhaps when I was not hearing his words as clearly as he intended me to, or, on occasion, trying to avoid them! Other diversionary excuses I made, but in that tone of hers that brooked no argument, she said, with finality: "Jesus, my son, you must do what is right, but you must also do what you can."

What can you do when your Heavenly Father and your earthly mother both conspire to tell you to do something? There is but one thing: you have to get on and do it! And so I sought out the groom's father and asked him to show me what wine he had left. He took me into their small and dusty storage room at the back of the property. Shrugging resignedly, he showed me the now-empty wine jars and wine skins. There really was not a drop left! My eyes scanned the storeroom; along one side were shelves filled with small pots and jars that he had made in his workshop; along the opposite wall stood six tall, old but sound earthenware jars. They gave me an idea of what I might do to help and, at the same time, to offer a deeper message. "Have your people fill these jars with water." It would take them a while to achieve this, which would give me the time I needed to prepare myself.

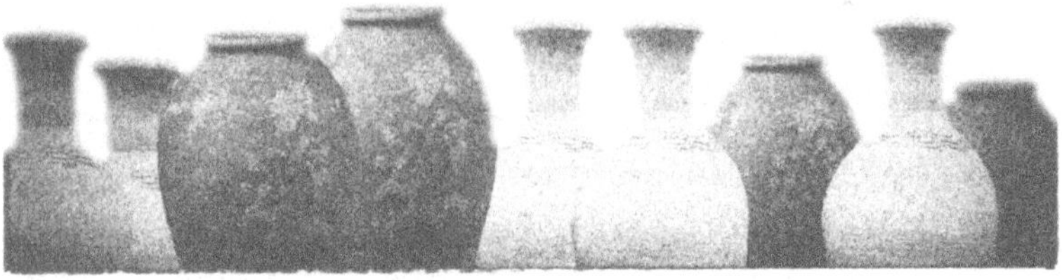

As they busied themselves filling the jars (I could see that both he and they were puzzled by my request, wondering how on earth it would help solve the problem, but, with faith, they complied). I sat on a small stool and watched the progress. As I sat, I offered prayers to my Father: *Heavenly Father, guide me this day. If this is my time to begin, help me to do your will. Help those who are here to see beyond the act. Make this the first step on their journey towards enlightenment.* Much sooner than anticipated, the jars were filled. I ushered everyone from the room; placing the lids on each of the jars, I now prayed aloud. "Mighty, glorious Father. Take this water and make it new wine; breathe body and richness into it. Make it a small reflection of your glory." The words themselves were not important; it was not a spell that I was casting! My Father, of course, knew already that which I desired, before I had even asked for it; my prayers were acknowledgement of that which I knew he would do.

Calling the groom's father back into the room, I drew him a small cup. He eyed it. He sniffed it. His eyes grew wider. He sipped it. And his jaw dropped. "How can I thank you?" he said, astounded. "This is the finest wine that I have ever tasted!" Hurriedly, he brought back his servants, had them fill jugs and tend to his guests. There was now plenty to go around; no small measures were needed!

Beforehand, I had told Mother that my time had not yet come. I was not sure that I had properly thought through delivering the various signs as I intended them. They were not done to impress for what they were but to deliver a far more important message. A much deeper message. So, I wondered what they would make of this. As I feared, most did not follow the thoughts through. They just thought Oh, Jesus is a good chap, somehow he has saved the family's blushes. They did not see the significance of the use of the jars set aside for holding water for ceremonial washing. They did not grasp that this signified the end of the water's life: when it is clean and fresh, it is drinkable, it is full of life, but when it has been used for cleansing feet, it is "dead", no longer of use and to be poured away. They did not read it as the first time I had talked of the resurrection: the water "dying" but then being resurrected as new wine! Because they were not ready, I did not think that I was ready. But I took something from this too. I saw that they would never be fully ready, would only be transformed to new wine after the culmination, and so waiting longer would brook no benefit. It was time to start. I saw it as clearly as I saw my reflection in the still water – wine – of those jars. One message they had received, however: as the guests all danced around in celebration, they lifted their voices to the Lord, singing His full-throated praises! Perhaps it did not matter that they had not grasped all the meanings; perhaps no one ever would. Perhaps it never would really matter!

SERMON PREPARATIONS

We sat in a tight circle around the fire, as the night was chill. Soon the time would come for me to give my first mass

outdoor sermon. Up until this point, I had only spoken to fairly small gatherings in synagogues, in houses, and occasionally in town plazas. Despite that knowing, I just could not decide upon a theme. I had prayed to my Father for guidance, but he had given me one of his more cryptic answers: *You will know it when you know it*! I had raised with my disciples yesterday the topic of the – well – topic! So, this night I was looking to them for ideas and suggestions, something that would at least spark further thoughts. "Moses had his Ten Commandments. Why don't you write yours?" suggested Peter. "Moses did not write them, and they are perfect; how could I match them?" I realised that my response sounded too harsh, so tried to soften it. "I mean to say, I'd like to find something new to talk about; something that will resonate because of its newness."

We continued debating ideas and themes. Fish came into the discussion; that felt good and something that we could build upon, but we did not quite manage to land it. Doing good deeds held promise, but we were not gifted with the right words to speak. Other topics were raised, some of which we debated for a good while; others came and were quickly rejected (although, strangely enough, I did return to two of those later in the year and they made for great topics!).

There was only the tiniest crescent of the waxing moon that night, but that meant that the stars blazed with a more fulsome glory; not only was the moon itself waxing, but it was waxing from that night's sky too and still we were no closer. For a while we sat in silence, our creativity exhausted. But then I came back to Peter's idea. "How about this: we map from the Ten Commandments, rather than trying to create a new set. So, rather than the *thou shalt not* approach, we talk about the *thou shalts* – Moses brought my Father's commands to the people; I will bring mine to match with them. I don't mean that I just state the opposites, of course; there is little sense in my saying *you should preserve life*, *you should speak only truthful words*, and so on – that adds nothing. But, how about making them reflective of a true catechism for life?" They had been nodding along with this, but I lost them with *catechism*. "I mean a design for life, how you approach the day-to-day."

We all seemed settled with the idea (perhaps some as they simply wanted to turn in for the night, of course!), and so I started to turn over a few ideas of how I might approach these. I was still getting agreement to my musings, but this next bit was on me. So I suggested that we all turn in for the night. I lay back beneath my blanket to watch the moon continue its slide from the heavens and the almost imperceptible swirl of the stars. Words rattled around inside my head; slowly I started joining them together. I didn't think that I would be getting any real sleep for what remained of that night.

SERMON ON THE MOUNT

Thin fingers of orange crept up through the morning sky. Those fingers grasped the horizon; they flexed and started to drag their huge bulbous body above that skyline. Dawn broke. And with the breaking, they came. Many, many races. Many, many creeds. Men and women. Young and old, children too. They all came. Talking in hushed tones or silently, they found space and seated themselves. My human part was truly amazed at how far people had travelled to see me, to meet with me. With the exception of the nomads, most of these people had rarely journeyed outside their own village, and yet, here they were, travelling three, four, or more, days, for perhaps no more than a glimpse!

Human fear arose within me: would I find the right words? Whilst the headlines were written, I needed to present them in a cohesive and engaging manner. But then I felt my Father's hand of reassurance upon my shoulder (as I always did), and I knew that the words would come. He had gifted me with the opening words: "Blessed are those who ..." We both knew that the rest would flow from that point. He opened my eyes and helped me to truly look around me: I looked to the left, and to the right; I saw many in the crowd in fear of that which the Romans might do; they had come despite that. They had come in defiance of their oppressors, but that did not overcome their fear and their nervousness as they looked around them. I looked also at the Romans who were scattered throughout the gathering; some overtly, in their soldiers' armour; some covertly, trying to blend in and listen in on conversations and reactions to my words. Suddenly, I knew which of the sections of my talk I should use first; I opened my lips, and from them, in whispered tones, tumbled the phrase: *blessed are the meek*.

I rose to my feet; as I rose, the hum of conversation receded until an expectant hush hung over the land. Even the noises of nature, the twittering of birds and other fauna, the quiet whisper of the wind, all these were stilled as though the whole world waited to hear that which I was about to say.

"My friends, bless you for being here to hear the words of our Father as we seek to draw nearer to Heaven. All glory to that Father on his heavenly throne. Blessed are all of you to be here and for being here. Blessed are those amongst you who are humble and modest in their doings. Blessed are those who do not seek to put themselves forward. Blessed are those who hold back. Blessed are those who show genuine deference. Blessed are those who are modest and respectful of all."

I let my voice rise in pitch and timbre: "Blessed are the meek! For they will become the inheritors of this earth!" I paused as a soft ripple ran through the crowd; this was not what those who had expected talk of rebellion (Roman or Jew) had anticipated; was I praising those who did not fight back? Was I commending a life of drudgery?

"Blessed are those who have lost someone near and grieve for them; I say to those of you who mourn that you will be comforted.

"Blessed are those who hunger and thirst for righteousness, for they will be filled beyond measure!

"Blessed are the merciful, for they in turn will be shown great mercy.

"I rejoice for those who are pure of heart, for they will see God, and in so doing will rejoice themselves.

"Most blessed are those who strive for peace; for those who are peacemakers will also be called children of God!

"Blessed, indeed, are those who are persecuted and maltreated for the perceived crime of righteousness, for, truly I say, their dwellings are prepared for them in the Kingdom of Heaven!"

By the fourth occasion, I made no preparations, we held no nighttime discussions, for I trusted wholly in my Father to guide my lips into speaking the right words. The themes on which I would speak remained constant for now; the words with which I explained them might differ in places. Those who flocked to see me, to hear from me, grew and grew; they were too many for the town, so on this occasion I climbed the mount in the east. Drawn by my spirit, with certainty they followed me. I reached an outcrop of rock, some seven cubits high; I scrambled up to its ledge and sat with my feet dangling down; smoothing down the cloth of my robe, I sat with my hands open in my lap whilst they assembled. I saw my closest disciples motioning for them to sit. As we had climbed, I had warned them that we might be here for some while. Slowly, the hubbub of voices subsided as thousands of eyes turned towards me, eyes of brown but also of hazel, of green, of grey, of blue, and also the milky white of those with no sight who had been led here by others. A solitary bird of prey wheeled above before racing off to the north. I let my eyes close, the better to see those who sat before me; I had prepared no words but had faith that they would come to me. I felt the myriad emotions of those who sat before me, sensing the reasons for their presence: the hurt, the brokenness, the heartache, the physical hurts; so too were there the curious, those who had come to support others. Drawing those hurts into me, I let them translate into the words that then came from my mouth; they were similar to those that I had uttered before. "Blessed are the submissive of spirit, for theirs is the Kingdom of Heaven, for the meek shall inherit the earth." None of them, nor any other human, were spiritually pure; for many their spirits strove to be pure, but each also had transgression (in the months to come, that part of me that was human transgressed also; there were times, through exhaustion, when that part of me wished the crowds away for solitude and rest). It was to those who accepted their misdeeds for what they were, those who did not seek to make excuses, that I spoke. That I did not give in to those temptations protected the half of me that was divine.

"When people insult you, persecute you and falsely level all kinds of evil against you because of me, rejoice! Be glad! Because great is your reward in Heaven; for in the same way they persecuted all the prophets who were before you. Many prophets sit amongst you now; the scrolls may not record their names, but wisdom and insight will spill from their lips."

The time for talk alone was coming to an end; soon my Father's power would also be shown through healing too.

ON THE TELLING OF STORIES

At first, I had told them in plain language what they must do. They nodded, pretending a wisdom that they did not feel. But I could see that they did not really understand. They acted as they did to the early Scriptures: they knew them by rote, could quote them word for word, and yet understood them not at all; the words were empty, emotionless. According to our original design, for us to tell you things would have been enough. You would have believed, trusted, as a child does, the words of their parents. But, when the evil one led you astray, and you ate of the Tree of Knowledge, that all changed. You learned to question, to doubt, to create alternative truths.

Don't get us wrong – it was never our intention that you lived a life of ignorance. We just wanted you to learn in proportion to your development; just as with one of your children, you don't try to teach them everything all at once! We tried to balance the evil that had been done through further gifts to you, such as conscience and free will. I think that they helped.

Telling was no longer enough. Reason and logic were needed; there was a need to engage your brains and let them reach their own conclusions. And so, I took the craft of storytelling and created a new branch of it, which I named the parable. These parables I told many times to many people. Those that I saw had been well received (I cannot say understood, as often they were not; but I saw a distance appear in the eyes of those who looked on.

I saw meaning – although not understanding – sink in), I would repeat more often. Some I used only once, for the opposite reason; those are not even recorded – although there is one exception. One of the aims of these was for them (and you) to see in images rather than just words.

This was particularly true for the disciples, I needed them to truly understand; they were the ones who would ensure that those words – and with them understanding – would spread across the globe and from generation to generation. Of course, they did not know that yet; I was not yet ready to tell them about my future – and neither were they ready to hear about it nor to understand it.

We were on a two-day trek now to our next destination, so as we walked, I made another attempt to explain the underlying need for parables.

It was late afternoon when we had arrived at our dwelling for that night, and they still did not seem any closer to understanding. I let some of my frustration show, driven by my human anger.

"You had ten instructions, yet you could not stick to them, though they were carved in stone! Moses was the first to speak of them, though others followed. But you did not listen! You did not hear! You carried those stones here and there in the wilderness; yet, you did not carry them in your hearts. And you ask me why I speak in parables! Perhaps, if you dwell on my words, your ears might be opened and the truth revealed. But you all have ears of cloth; they flap around this way and that. They hear the salacious, and they hold onto it. They hear rumours, and they share them. They hear lies, yet they retell those same lies. And yet they cannot hear the Word when it is spoken right next to them!"

All my disciples sat around in puzzled silence, shocked at my outburst! I knew that today's parables had taxed their understanding; my anger was unjust – but such is the nature of that emotion. One of them, especially, had troubled them: I had portrayed a master going away for a protracted period; he had left one servant with ten bags of gold (which he had managed wisely and doubled the amount by the time of his master's return); a second he had given five bags, which had become ten by the time he returned. The third servant he had given one bag of gold; this servant feared his master's wrath, and so he did not want to risk losing the money, so he buried it to keep it safe. This had really had them scratching their heads.

It was Thomas who broke the silence and voiced that which they were all thinking: "Lord, you have spoken many times of the meek inheriting the earth; of he who is last being first; of not clamouring for the best seats at a wedding celebration. And yet this seems to argue the opposite? How can this be?"

They were now all sitting in rapt attention, waiting for an answer – some even wondering if I had got the story back to front!

"So, the master gifted them with gold?" Heads nodded. "And those who used that gift wisely returned it twofold?" More nodding. Then I took a sidestep, which initially confused them further: "Matthew, where did your skill with numbers come from?" Without hesitation, he told me, "That gift came from God!" I turned to Simon, "And Simon, from whence came your great strength?" "From the Lord, of course!"

I waited a few moments to see if the denarius might drop, although I knew it would not.

"And when you were brawling in bars, Simon, were you using that strength wisely?" He hung his head in answer, mumbling "No, Lord." A further pause. But this time, Matthew had started to grasp towards the answer: "So, you are speaking of how wisely a gift is used? It would have been wiser for the third servant to invest the money, although the amount was smaller than that held by the others?"

I nodded, pleased that it had not taken further prompting. "Just so." I raised a finger towards Heaven. "And in the days that come, after I am gone, other gifts will be given to you, and indeed to many. Gifts of speaking words which are truly understood, gifts of healing, gifts of compassion, gifts of truly communicating with the young, gifts of hearing the words of my Father and with the ability to share them with those who have ears, and so many more besides. This, then, is your choice: to squander those gifts, to make personal profit from them. Or to use them for good works, to share the word and spread our gospel, the good news, to help those who need it most.

"Or you could waste them fighting and doing conjurer-like healings in a bar!

"When I return, should I not reward those who have used their gifts wisely over those who have not?"

Whilst they did nod in comprehension of these words, still they did not understand about my "going away". They pictured a voyage of some kind. Not death. Only time would teach them the nature of that journey.

"The gifts received may be smaller for some and greater for others. But whatever the gift, even the least, use that gift wisely; do not squander it. Do not bury it. Rejoice in it. Share it. Use it; for the greater glory of our Father." Finally, they had grasped it. I hoped they would remember it in the days and years ahead; that when the time came, they would use those gifts – without hesitation, without fear, without internal debate.

Later that evening, I set off for a walk in the gloaming of nightfall. I'd thought that I would be alone; I'd thought the disciples and the women were all busy helping our hosts to prepare our evening meal. But as I walked, I saw Thomas ahead; he was deep in thought. "Thomas?" He looked up, awoken from his walking reverie. "Ah! Lord! I was thinking on some of the parables that you have told us." I smiled to myself, pleased that perhaps this approach was working. "You told us one time of a rich man who was not able to give away all his belongings to help the poor and to follow you; I remember you saying, 'It is easier for a camel to go through the eye of a needle…' Now, I know (at least, I think that I know) that the parables that you tell are made up illustrations to help us to understand, but I still cannot help but feel sorry for this fellow." Further worry passed across his face. "At least, I had assumed that they did not concern actual people; if I am wrong, then it is perhaps even worse! That poor man!"

I rested my hand upon his shoulder. "Real or imagined, who can say? Perhaps I should finish the story? There is certainly more to that story. It tells how my words had sowed a seed with that man, and later he did indeed give it all away and set up a refuge for the poor in his home. He is following me spiritually rather than physically. Yes, Thomas, I knew that then the time was not right for him, but now the time is right for him, the veil has been lifted, and he can see clearly. The scrolls might not record his name, but in my Father's House his name appears."

We walked in silence for a while, I could see that he was absorbing this and that he was readying his next question. “But are riches not a reward from Heaven? Just as poverty and pain are a punishment from Heaven? Certainly, the Torah talks about rewards, riches from heaven for doing that which is good and right!” “For me, being rich is neither reward nor punishment – both can saddle one with problems, albeit of a different nature. I think maybe we need a new word here; I’ll have to think of something that works. Sure, riches can mean money, property, livestock. But in the context of the true Torah (rather than the way that it is translated by some), riches are more to do with spiritual contentment. One who is blessed with a stillness of their soul, whose heart is filled with a rich warmth.

“The man who has financial wealth finds it hard to question that wealth. It is rare for a rich man to ask, ‘why am I wealthy?’ They do not think further than that they are content. But the poor man! The poor man will often question his lot, especially when he sees the rich man. But can you not see that the poor man can also be content? He will see the blessings that are around him, the beauty of the world in which he lives; he will see the companionship that he has; he will offer praises for his family; he will show gratitude for that which he does have, not envy for that which he does not possess!”

In later years you guys tried to read far, far too much into the stories that I told. You would dissect and analyse every single word; you would say, wisely nodding your heads, *Ah, I see what he has done here; this means this and that means that*, and yet, on most levels, my parables were only simple in their meaning: often they had but one meaning. Sadly, I have to report, that you totally overlooked the overall context and focused instead simply on the individual words that made up the parable, not the meaning that I intended for the listener (and for you in those subsequent years as the reader) to gain from that which I said. Sure, I added in reference points and the familiar to help in the telling of those tales, to give the listener places of comfort in the listening. Sometimes, those things did support the overall meaning, but they were lesser in the tale, not equal or greater.

Later that evening, I overheard John, Peter, Luke and Bartholomew speaking amongst themselves. "He's such a great teacher," said Peter. "I've listened to many, many teachers, and hardly any of them ever made any sense to me at all. I would listen intently; I would think on what they had said, and yet I walked away sometimes more confused than when I had entered the temple or the synagogue! I was starting to think that it was just me not being very bright. And yet Jesus tells one simple story and it makes such sense deep in the core of me, deep, deep within my heart I understand!" I smiled to myself so pleased to hear this endorsement of how I tried to teach not just my disciples but all those who came to listen to things that I had to say.

The next evening, prompted by a question posed by Judas, our discussions turned to man being made in God's image. Judas had said, "Master, it is said that we are created in God's image. And yet I am in appearance very different to Matthew, and to the others, particularly Bartholomew; so, which of us most closely resembles God?" I suspected, strongly, that Judas was hoping for the answer *you are*, but it was true of all of them, and indeed none of them! "Let's think of it this way. My Father created you in his image, in his image he created you. That doesn't, of course, mean that you are an exact mirror but an image or an impression – or maybe a representation might be the best word. You are all like each other, and yet unalike. Consider the sheep or the fishes: to many, all the sheep look alike, as do the fishes. And yet to the shepherd, or the fisherman, their differences are myriad. So, they are the same, yet different.

"So too, just like Him, you have a spirit. Of course, not as powerful; He created the world and everything in it, whereas your creations are of a smaller scale – I do not mean that they are less, just that they are different! Some of you are clever with rope; making the rope in the first place, and then creating fishing nets from it, boat rigging, and more. In my time, I became skilled in working wood. There are some of you who can create art, or music, or poetry; perhaps pottery, or wine, or clothing; or a thousand other skills that He has gifted you with (every single one of us has been gifted with something, although, sadly, not everyone discovers all of their talents). It is your spirit that helps you to create; maybe you have had those moments where you have created something, and you say that you have no idea where the inspiration comes from? That is, with certainty, a time when your spirit, and His Spirit, are connecting.

"You might say my spirit is stronger than yours, but I am not sure that is quite right, the spirit is beyond strength; perhaps it is that I am more in tune with mine? And I have the added advantage that I can also call upon my Father's Spirit – as indeed can you, although sometimes that is harder for you, not always will you succeed, but it is there for everyone: there are days and there are days!"

They seemed in the mood for talking that night; not a one of them seemed to be sleepy – which made a change. The night had grown still and silent outside; our lamps had started to burn low, their olive oil consumed; but the fire still burned brightly in its pit, casting dancing orange-hued shadows across the roughly whitewashed walls of the house. Our hosts still sat with us, absorbing every word, but they sat silently, as though fearing that if they spoke, we would suddenly be reminded of their presence and send them from the room so that (as they saw it) we could speak of lofty things; things beyond their ken. Which was of course not true; I never objected to anyone listening to our words. In fact, I welcomed it; nothing pleases me more than an open mind.

ON GOOD AND EVIL

It was a chill cloudless night; a million million stars pricked night's black velvet. Their light, too, was cool. We sat in a tight circle around the fire, bathed in its warming orange light. Softly, we talked of the wonders of that day.

A log on the fire split with a loud crack, rupturing the stillness of the night; as though summoned by the sound, a scorpion scurried into our midst. With a speed that belied his frame, Simon's staff whipped down on its back; the scorpion twitched once and then was still. "Evil little critter!" "My Father did not say so," I offered.

The flickering flames now illuminated several blank faces. Simon's voice spoke for them all: "How so?" "Remember your Torah," I gently instructed. "What does the twenty-fourth verse of the first scroll tell us?" Matthew was the first to speak the words that they were all seeking to draw from their memories: "Then God said, 'Let the earth be filled with animals. And let each produce more of its own kind. Let there be tame animals and small crawling animals and wild animals. And let each produce more of its kind.'"

"And how does that section conclude?" I probed. "'God looked at everything that He had made, and saw that it was very good. Evening passed, and morning came. This was the sixth day.'"

I nodded approval. "So, my Father looked at *everything* that he had made and declared it very good, didn't he? I know that some might argue that he meant the animals were good, but that it was man who was very good; that is a moot point! He did not say 'everything that I have created is very good, except for scorpions'. Or, 'except for frogs, because they are slimy!' No, His declaration was that everything was indeed good. All have their place. All have their purpose; even the huge beasts of the sea. Only the Father can create; the Evil One can only corrupt, coerce, confine, and confuse. Animals contain no malice; they act from hunger, they act from instinct, they act for defensive reasons. Only man has the knowledge of good and evil."

Thomas voiced that which they were all thinking: "But how can that which kills be good?" I paused, then: "But all men kill; are all men evil? Are *you* evil, Thomas?" "But I have never killed!" he cried. "Not ever," I asked? "Not even the smallest thing crawling on the ground, by error? Or the insect that bites, by intention?"

He had no response, so I went on: "Only the Father knows all. Only He understands the balance of all things. All things are created good, but only man is intentionally evil; only man has eaten of the tree of the knowledge of good and evil, and therefore truly knows what he does; the animals do not know these things! They do what is natural to them, that is part of their design, their nature."

A silence descended as they digested my words. Another lesson had been learned; they did not fully understand it yet, but I saw that they each now considered my words and their implications. Comprehension would take time.

The fire spat and hissed, the logs mimicking the sounds of the serpent, the sounds that he would now be making, as further comprehension grew. His life was so much easier when such pronouncements as the one uttered by Simon, originally, went unchallenged.

“Sleep now,” I commanded. “May your dreams bring further insights. Tomorrow will bring another full day, with little time for reflection.”

John placed a few more logs on the fire; they would be sufficient to keep us warm until the morning.

JAMES AND THE BLIND MAN

Not long after that, we arrived in the town of Bethsaida, where my disciples had been out in the town spreading the word; James brought a blind man to me, with a petition for his healing. To help me to focus on my prayers for this, I took him to the outskirts of the town; here it was quieter, although still some of the townsfolk were milling around, curious to see what would happen.

I calmed myself and opened a brief, silent prayer; it was the one I nearly always used on these occasions: *Wonderful Father, help me to do what is right for this man.*

I felt my hands grow warmer. In some places where I had healed, there was not always a ready source of water. Water represented an important part of the healing process for me; whilst it was only symbolic, it represented a washing clean. It also represented the Waters of Life: the mighty rivers of Eden. So, I had grown used to using my own saliva for this purpose, which I now did. I spat on my thumbs and immediately pressed them to his eyes, beginning my second prayer, which I murmured aloud: "Lord, Blessed Father, if it be Your will, allow me to heal this man. Bring sight to his eyes; bring healing to his heart; bring, too, sight to his heart so that he truly sees you! I pray for this in Your precious name, not mine." I pressed slightly harder for a few moments and then removed my hands from his face.

I could feel the healing energy of creation tingling in my fingertips as I remade his health anew; placing those fingertips on his long-closed eyes, I felt but one spark leap across the minute gap. But it was enough; his eyelids flickered and then opened. They closed again, hurriedly, as the initially painful light flooded in. “Open your eyes; tell me what you see,” I commanded.

He was beyond excited: “I see grey shapes! They are moving around! They look like trees! Lord, thank you!”

But I was not satisfied; yes, his sight was restored somewhat, but he was not fully healed. “May I pray one more time, please?” I asked. He nodded acquiescence. I repeated the process and my prayer, saying it twice. I was then silent for some time, adding a further silent prayer. Finally, I removed my thumbs and again asked him what he saw. For a few moments, it seemed that he had been struck dumb; his jaws moved, but no sound came. Finally, he spoke. Well, at first it was just a roar of praise: “Hallelujah! Hallelujah!” He grasped my hands in his. “Thank you, thank you, thank you, thank you, thank you, thank you, thank you! Now I see clearly! Everything is clear! I see you, I see the people around us! I see the houses, the trees, the sky, the birds – the beautiful birds – they fly through a sky that is rich and blue!” He gabbled on for a long while, and I let him. Finally, he finished his exultations. “I must tell my friends!” “No, say nothing of me, please,” I asked him. I wanted the people to come to hear my words, to be enlightened, to follow my ways. Not to simply bring ailments and then to wander off, healed of their afflictions but still empty, unhealed in their hearts. Of course, I ached to heal the world of all afflictions, but that day had not yet come. My task, for now, was to give but a taste of the time when heaven would return to the earth, the Garden be remade anew, and the New Day begin. How I longed for that day! My Father knew when that day would come, but He did not share that detail with me then: it might have diverted me from my path.

Later that evening, as we sat around our fire pit as we usually did (although this night, we sat in the courtyard of one of the houses, as invited guests), I reflected on that blind man. Whilst the power and authority to heal came from my Father, it had always happened fully; it had not been partially withheld. I wondered now if that initial partial healing was also a message to my disciples: now you are starting to see, but you do not yet see clearly. You see the shapes, you see darker and lighter, but you do not truly see. That afternoon as we walked through the village, I asked those around me who people thought I might be. Some had answered John, some had suggested Elijah, others had just used the word prophet. Peter, for the first time, had called me Messiah, but truly, he saw only the grey and blurred shape; he did not fully see me as I am. I would have to die and then live again for that veil to be finally lifted. Perhaps Father had a lesson for me also: don't make it routine; make sure the focus is on whole healing, not just on the symptoms presented.

At the fringes of the crowd, something was happening. I tried to move towards it. But the crowd pressed in around me. Through snatches of shouted conversations, I gathered what had gone on. Roman legionaries had tried to disperse the crowd, but one had become over-zealous and stabbed one of the women with his short sword. As I edged closer, I saw her on the ground, blood spreading out in the dirt around her, drying almost instantly on the hot sand. Her husband lay across her, seeking to staunch the blood. It was too late for her; the wound was too deep. I knew that I could have called her back, knew that it was within my power. But I felt my Father's hand on my shoulder, heard him saying to me, "No, my Son, her time to rise again has not yet come. Stay your hand. It will be revealed in time why some must go, whilst others must wait behind." I knew that to which he referred, one of the greatest of secrets; I knew nearly all, except the time. That, only he knew. The time. I just knew it was not yet. But that did not quell the flame that had ignited in my human heart. The flame of rebellion. I wanted to scream out "Why?" I wanted to defy him. I wanted just this once for my will to be done. I clenched my fists. But then, washed by new understanding, I relaxed them again.

I suppose that you could say that I now had knowledge of rebellion and how it made for at least a part of the hearts of men, but now, that knowledge grew, became physical, came to life as I felt it flare in my human heart. I knew that I must deny it. But that did not make it easier. I wanted to heal the whole world; my human side was so desperate for that. But it was not the time. I did not know the time, only my Father knew that, but I did know that this was not it. I had to keep repeating that to myself, to keep it uppermost. The tears, the pleas of the crowd and of my own followers scourged me like whips. My own tears joined them as we wept for a life cut short.

THE PEOPLE COME TO ME

We had been guests in the town for three days now; from dawn until way after dusk people sought us out. We did not even need to step beyond the courtyard to pursue our mission. Whilst we had not declared them as such, those who came approached me through the eastern portico of the courtyard, using it as the entrance. They then left through the one on the western side. The queues of people continued to come, they grew greater every day: the blind, the mute, the lame, some with minor ailments (but they were important to them, and therefore important to me), and so I healed them all. James and John fretted over those with mild ailments too. On the third day of our residence, and of my healing surgeries, they came to me. I was touched that they had noticed the toll it was taking on me and that their words were meant to be supportive.

They did their usual double act when it came to talking:

“Lord,”

“We’ve been thinking.”

“There are so many who wish to come to you.”

“But many trouble you with trifling things.”

“Let us talk to them as they wait.”

"Let us move on those who do not really need to see you."

"For most, their problems will resolve themselves."

"They don't need to see you!"

I let them talk on for a little longer before raising my hand to speak: "James, John, I am very grateful for the thoughtfulness and care that you are showing towards me; I know that your motives are well-meaning. These things may seem minor to you, but they mean much more to those who come to me. Think of the fellow who came to us yesterday; he suffered 'only' from a non-defiling rash to his back, yet its impact on him was great. It is not for us to judge; it is for us to help as we can."

They had accepted this – albeit reluctantly – but still sought for something to lighten my burden. Now, they started to usher away the small children; those who did not yet count in this adult world. As the children passed near to me, towards the western exit, I lowered an arm to block their passage. I plucked one of them up, setting the child upon my knee. I cried in a loud voice (as I wanted those outside to hear too): "Exult this little one! You must be more like him – a child, open to learning and instruction. Not closed and set in his ways as you are! You are all children, yet you know it not. You pretend that you are other than how you are! A child's eyes are wide, absorbing all. A child's heart is clean; yours are now stained, some fully corrupted; your eyes are hooded, seeing only that which you wish to. To you, a child does not matter until they are grown into a man or a woman, but to our Father, they matter far more than do you. Be more like them. Just accept things as they are told. Do not question; do not doubt. For when a father says to their child, this is how so-and-so is, then their child does not ask for more, they take it to their heart. They do not question."

Some while back, now, when we had first arrived in Bethsaida, I had healed a lame man. He had been waiting at a colonnaded well, which was reported to have healing waters (nonsense, of course!). I had healed him of his lameness and also of the sin of unforgiveness that was anchored in his heart.

I sent him on his way with an instruction to sin no more. That night, I had spoken long with my Father in prayer. I was starting to worry that I might, in some cases, be healing the outer hurt but leaving inner hurts and, with them, the door to sin open. Or, perhaps worse, not giving healing to the man who glorified the Father in his heart but who did not come forward; might that lack of healing not turn his heart from the Lord? *Ah, my Son, you must remember that all these healings are but temporary. It is not until the day when time ends that healings will be for all and*

will be permanent. Remember Job – he lost everything, suffered physical hurt, but his belief never wavered.

At the middle of the day, my disciples dismissed the crowd so that we might eat, so that I could rest, and also so that I could pray. As we neared the end of the repast, I felt my Father's hand again upon my shoulder; it gently nudged me in a certain direction. As I followed his guidance, I came to a woman standing on the periphery of the crowd. She had a red shawl around her head and yet loose auburn hair tumbled from it (it was a hint, and a suggestion, of that which she offered); my Father often guided me towards the lost. "Sister," I said to her, "come with me; follow a new path." She looked up into my eyes, and a hint of a smile crossed her lips. "But, Lord," she declared, "I have gone too far down this particular path to ever turn around." "Not so, it is never too late to return and follow a new path." Gently I took her by the hand and led her towards the place where we were staying. That same night as we walked through the emptying streets, we passed (as I knew we would) a tax collector closing up his booth and ready to return home for the night. He saw me. He knew who I was. He cast his eyes towards the ground. He knew her too. He paid her taxes. She paid him nothing; well, rather, she paid him with favours. Of course he didn't take her taxes from his own pocket! He charged others extra on their taxes and put those towards hers. As we drew alongside him, I said to him, "You should join us this evening and share a meal." Involuntarily, his gaze left the dusty path. He looked at me incredulously; his eyebrows shot up. "Me, join you?" "Yes, in my Father's House there is room for all those who turn from one path and start upon a new one." You could almost see the physicality of the change as new hope came to him: his shoulders became less rounded, his gaze less furtive. He spoke no more words until much later that evening, but careless of even locking his booth, like Matthew all those months previously, he followed in our wake.

Perhaps prompted by this final comment, later on that day, Peter asked, "Come the day when Heaven comes down to earth, won't it be very crowded?" "Not at all, for in my Father's House there are many rooms! Mind you," I added, "as soon as I talk like that it probably confuses you more. The *rooms* will not be rooms as you picture them now. Things will be so different then. There will be no more sickness, no more death, no weeping, no pain; indeed, there will be no sleeping and no waking! The space that we occupy will be different. The world will not be as the world we know; we will live in a New Jerusalem, a new place beyond space, beyond time even." Blank faces stared back at me. They were still struggling with parables; this was clearly a step too far. I let it rest and returned to simpler conversations.

SENDING OUT THE TWELVE

Last night, they had all gone early to their rest. Some of that exhaustion stemmed from being in the same place for several days. They had grown used to our nomadic lifestyle. I had sat alone in the courtyard for a long while after they had retired. An orchestra of insects had serenaded me: their clicks and chirps, their humming and buzzing, their screeches and sighs rising and falling in crescendos and calandos. It was time for us to do a new thing, but I had not yet coalesced my thoughts as to what that new thing might be – of course, I needed to seek Father's guidance too.

The discussions that we had been having during recent days finally convinced me: it was time to let the disciples experience the world for themselves; for them to carry the word as they would have to when I would not be alongside them every day. They had matured so much, in so many ways; sure, there were still many rough edges, but this trial would soften many of those. I also felt the impact of the busyness myself, with all those that I was ministering to, healing, saving, and with the subsequent demands of my disciples wanting their own time with me, and for me to instruct or to explain to them further on what had happened during the day. This was to the extent that I did not always get to spend my own quiet time with my Father each day as I wanted to, as I needed to. That time of prayer is as important to me as it is to you. And so, as we broke our fast that morning, I told them what I had in mind.

I had been sitting quietly in a corner whilst our host and her cousin had busied themselves preparing a breakfast. The warm, comforting aroma of baking bread filled the air; it mingled with the pungence of the herbs that they had mixed into some of the dough. A jug of freshly drawn water and a jug of freshly expressed goat's milk were standing on the table. It was that time of year when only dried fruits were to be had, but there was a bowl of these, together with a few almonds.

They all still kept the hours of fisher-folk, and trades people (even Matthew had adapted his sleeping and waking pattern to fit with theirs), so, as the sun commenced its ascent of the skies, they too were rising. Simon-Peter came first to the table; often his temper was short in the morning, but this morning he was positively cheery! James and John were next, together as always. For this task, I would be pairing them off, but these two I should split up, I thought to myself; it would help both with their independence. Judas was hot on their heels, as though not wanting to miss out on anything. A few moments later and Matthew had joined the table; he was tidy, well groomed – unlike Peter, whose hair was tousled and whose clothes were crumpled, as though he had slept in them (which he had!). And then came the rest, all together, probably as they had all had to share the same room. They were holding a light-hearted debate over which of them snored the loudest.

The bread was now being set on the table; taken straight from the oven, a haze of heat could be seen above it when Peter drew back the cloth that had capped the basket. I smiled to myself over how they passed the bread around, tearing off chunks for each other, looking after each other. It was a tiny but significant change from the first days when they had simply grabbed for themselves. They had set a place for me too and placed bread and fruit on my plate alongside a cup of water and a cup of milk. I hurried to join them, driven by a human desire for warm, fresh bread. For a while we busied ourselves with the important task of eating; there was only minimal conversation. I tore hungrily at the bread, breaking off a large chunk and savouring its taste; such a simply flavoured staple, not much more than flour and some simple herbs, and yet all the more delicious for it! I let the mellow mustiness of the milk slide down my throat, washing the crumbs of the bread, laced with those herbs, along with it.

Hunger sated, the conversation turned to what we would be doing that day. I sensed their insouciance towards another day of ministry within the town, but also their resignation to its necessity. So, I immediately had their attention when I told them that today it was time for us to begin a new thing. I continued: "It is time that you each take a separate path to spread my word. I intend to send you out from here each on a different pathway; you will take with you my words, you will spread the good news, you will heal, you will cast out demons."

Around the table, I sensed conflicting emotions: excitement, fear, wonder, trepidation; there were personal doubts too: were they worthy of my trust.

For a few moments, silence reigned, But then the hubbub of questions began:

"What should we take with us?"

"Surely you do not mean for us to travel alone?"

"But how will we heal?"

"Where will we go, in which direction?"

In turn, I gave my responses, before a more detailed outline.

"Take very little with you."

"No, you will not go alone, you will go in pairs!"

"A greater measure of the Holy Spirit, I will give you for a short while."

"You will head north-east, east, south-east, south, south-west, and west along the coastline."

"Many difficulties lie before you, although they are but a taste of the difficulties to come when I am gone from you. These journeys will not be easy, although the full persecution of my words has not yet begun; indifference you will meet; you will meet both the hospitable and the inhospitable.

"These commands I do give you: you must love your enemies; if the welcome that you are given is not as it should be, then simply shake the dust off your feet and move on – there will be many others who do have ears that wish to hear. Stay in one dwelling when you are in a town, do not go from house to house; that way, you will know when the time comes to move on. Scatter my words like seeds; some of those seeds will take immediate root, some will root after a while, some will lie fallow and wither. You will learn, as you help others to learn." I was trying to prepare them for that which they were about to face, but also that which they would face in the future. Advice poured from me; it was as though I was trying to baptise them with words – but that was not the baptism that they needed. Looking around them, I saw from their faces that they had absorbed all that they could for now.

I divided them into their pairs; I did not wish for those pairings to be a safe coupling. I split up those who were often together; I put together those with opposing outlooks. Through those mismatches I sought to show a future where all differences would be cast out.

The gift of the Holy Spirit, in full measure, I gave them for this short while; a taste of that which was to come. I laid my hands on each of them in turn. That passing of my Spirit into them said more than a million of my words could have done. With no more words, each pair set out as soon as they had received my gift. Now that the last pair had gone, it was my turn to leave too. I headed for the mountains; it was a time for me to be alone, a time for reflection.

THE HOLY SPIRIT

When the twelve returned, they were overflowing with joy at all that they had achieved: healings, casting out demons, offering succour, teachings, and more besides. I would have liked them to write down the stories of those journeys, as I am certain that they would be encouraging to you, but that did not happen – they wanted only to tell my story when the time came for writing. Whilst we had set no time for their return, the spirit residing in them drew them back when the time had come. I had spent seven days on the mountain, meditating at its summit, then I had returned to the town; there were many households that I wished to visit. The disciples journeyed for eighty days; on the eighty-first day they all returned. By midday, we were all together once more.

They had so many questions about the Holy Spirit, so it seemed a good point to have another stab at explaining Him to them (and to you) again. As we sat at the table that evening, the room illuminated with the flickering light of the oil lamps, I made a start: "The Holy Spirit is a manifestation of our love, my Father's and mine, for you. God's love for you, for the world, and for everything in it became so strong that it became somewhat tangible. When He saw you, and all your imperfections (small and large), He loved you even more than He knew He would when first he conceived of you! God the Father, of course, came first. Which came second is harder to speak through, as it happened outside time; so, in many ways the three came as one, although in other ways there was a very clear order. Sorry, I know this probably isn't helping. But I am constricted by your language and the words within it. You have half myths about the number of different words that Eskimos and the Inuit have for snow – in fact, the Scots may have more, depending how you count them! (Is a synonym a different word? Of course it is!) Just to scrape the surface of these three, as it were, I can think of: aprilsnö, åsksnö, blin-drift, cahki, ciegar, feefle, flindrikin, glush, ground-gru, guoldu, hjarn, kafald, kafaldi, kafsnjór, kramsnö, krap, lappvante, mjöll, moarri, modd, skava, skavvi, skelf, slabb, snær, snaw-broo, snaw-ghast, sneesl, snjór, snow-smoor, soavli, vahca. Now that's the kind of breadth of vocabulary that I need to help me here!"

I looked at their completely blank faces, and realised that I had entirely lost them: Scots and Eskimos meant nothing to them (it probably means more to you, as you read this)! Snow was a word they knew, but mostly as something far off. I started again: "Sorry, it is not that snow has anything to do with it; it is just an illustration. It is with other words where I need that breadth! Love tops that list of words, of course; the Greeks have helpfully added further definitions: eros, philia, erotoropia, storge, philautia, pragma, agape. The spirit is all of those types of love, and others besides."

I tried something visual: I held up a stick and broke it. Then I held forth two sticks, which did not break: "Two are stronger than one." Finally, I took the cord from around my waist, a cord made of three strands, and lifting it high, I held it taut between my two hands, stretched above my head, my feet I planted wide apart. I let some of my strength be seen in the stance. That power, an echo of my spirit, I put, too, into my voice: "Yet bind three together, one plus one plus the Father and it is unbreakable!" It was a step in the right direction; the practical demonstration had at least made some sense to them. I thought that it was enough for one day, so I finished with: "Here is my final word for you on this for now: the Spirit is also the glue that makes the Father and me one. Indeed, it is the Spirit that makes He and I and all of you one."

EATING ON THE SABBATH

Despite its being the Sabbath, I felt that it was time to move on. I wasn't sure what prompted my urgency, but I had roused everyone and led them out before they had even had the chance to break their fast. Now, in addition to the twelve, a number of women had joined our happy little group. At first, the men had spoken against this, but I had teased them into submission by implying that they were worried that the women would outpace them and walk for longer!

We were heading somewhat towards the east. It had been dark as we had set off – the moon had slipped behind the horizon, so we had only the light of the stars to guide us. Now a thin line of orange started to appear on the horizon; below it were the shadowy purples and blacks of the mountains; above it were the dark blues and blacks of the sky. Behind us, in an oblique line to our left, I was aware that we were followed, but not by our usual followers. No, this was a melange of Pharisees and Sadducees. I suspected that they did not come to listen to my words; well, perhaps they did want to hear me speak, but only in the hope that they might ensnare me if I spoke wrongly!

It was not a long walk to the next town. The town that we had left behind was known mainly as a trading post; the one that we headed towards was a farming town. Almost as soon as we had passed beyond the last dwelling of the old town, we had entered a rough wilderness; there had been no softening of the edges between town and wild. This was not so as we approached our destination: some way out, we started to see neat farmland fields; some were grassed and housed sheep and goats, but most were arable and held crops that were near to being ready for harvesting. The outer fields had been spread out, with rough ground between them, so we had wended a path between them. Now, as noon approached, and we drew nearer the city, only the thinnest of margins separated one field from another. On both sides of us now were crops of corn, their heads heavy and drooping. Who can say which of us started it, but soon we were all plucking off ears of corn, rubbing off the coarse outer husks and popping the soft seeds into our mouths; it was the first sustenance that we had taken that day.

Those who had followed us had by now come much closer. One of them called out: "Why are you journeying on the Sabbath? Why are you doing what is not right and reaping corn on the Sabbath?" Several of the disciples started to apologise to me for breaking the Sabbath, thinking that I would be cross with them. But my retort was for the Pharisees and Sadducees: "Why are *you* journeying on the Sabbath? And what code is it that we are breaking by eating this simple food on this day?" Thinking that they had me cornered, their leader, all swagger and overflowing with pomposity, snapped: "We journeyed to catch you breaking the rules and we have done so: it is forbidden to harvest on the Sabbath!"

"Plucking a few ears of corn does not really constitute harvesting! Did I not see one of you stoop down just now to pluck a small pebble from their sandal? Would that not, then, constitute quarrying?" He raised a fleshy, accusatory finger to admonish me, but before he could speak, I forged on: "Does journeying as a spy still not classify itself as journeying? Or is it your contention that rules may be broken to catch someone else breaking the rules? Hypocrite!"

We marched on, leaving him fuming and feeling humiliated. It gave me no pleasure to hold such debates; it was my hope, of course, that such discussions might bring revelation. But I knew that in this case that would not be so, he would be another in the queue to bring me to harm in some way or other.

Nor was I seeking to be rebellious myself; I wholly accept the precept of Sabbath. We all need that day of rest; working seven days without rest, indeed working harder and harder, for naught more than money (or things) is entirely meaningless. I was there to walk you all towards eternal Sabbath, eternal rest, where you have all that you *need* and care no longer about that which you *want*.

Arriving at our next destination revealed a further gripe and more shock and outrage amongst the Sadducees and Pharisees. Here, they took exception that I was followed also by women, who I treated as equally as the men who followed me! They quoted selective pieces of scripture to show me where I was at best misguided and at worse wilfully arrogant (as they saw it). I did not waste time bandying further words with them; we just got on with our mission: we shared the good news, I spoke further parables, we healed.

I had healed many that were blind. There was a symbolism to it: I wanted to remove the blindness from the many, the blindness that sought to blot out the sins of the world. Would that I could cure the Pharisees and Sadducees of their blindness! But their blindness is internal, goes deeper, and they do not know it. I cannot force myself upon them. I will heal only if I am asked to. That is a start of faith: the recognition of my authority and the means by which I do these things. In the same way, there were so many, too, who were deaf. Words would waft towards their ears, tickle their eardrums, but would not be truly *heard.* Those words would not pass through and into conscious thought. Often now when I spoke, I would finish with: "He who has eyes, let him see; he who has ears, let him hear!" It was a prayer over them all.

OF THE SOWING OF SEEDS

This village seemed particularly deaf to my words; whilst they did come to listen, I convinced only very few. I wondered if something more demonstrable might work for them. On this particular day, we had moved a short way outside the village, to allow more people to gather. We were in a partially cleared field, not wanting to cause any damage in a planted one. Here and there, a few weeds remained to be cleared; there were also many stones that still needed to be removed; against the low stone wall, which marked the perimeter, bags of seed stood waiting to be planted. These observations planted the germ of an idea for the content of today's talk.

They had all positioned themselves in the western half of the field, some on the bare earth, others on reed mats that they had brought with them. I was standing to the east, the sun at my back warming me through the cloth of my robe – not that it was a cold morning. The ground was dry, so as they had walked to find their places, they stirred up a haze of dust, which hung now in the air above them; it made the crowd look somewhat like an impressionistic painting. A silence descended as they waited for me to speak; those who had come to descry my messages poised with tablets to write notes upon; those who had come to snare me poised to whisper disparaging words to those around them; those who had come to learn, attentive. I picked up one of the bags of seed, hefting it into place as a sower would. "A farmer went out into his fields to sow." I reached into the sack and pulled out a generous handful of seed, this I scattered along the path that ran parallel with the wall; twice more I scattered seed along the path. "But, some of those seeds fell along a path. And guess what! The birds came and ate those seeds!" As if on cue, a dozen and a half sparrows descended greedily onto the seeds that I had scattered; they were seemingly oblivious to the many people seated on the ground and set about feasting and feeding themselves on the seeds, happily twittering away.

I moved further into the field, leaving them to their meal. Human eyes followed me to see what came next; avian eyes followed me, wondering if there would be more easy breakfast to follow. I scooped up more seed from the sack. "Some of the seed fell amongst the rocks." In a section of the field not yet cleared of rocks and stones, I scattered several more handfuls. This was all too much for the field owner, who leaped up in anger, seeing red at this waste of his recently purchased seed! On my periphery, I saw one of my disciples, Judas, probably, press a coin into his hand and whisper, "The loss is but small, this will cover it." It seemed to work, as he sat down, mollified – perhaps he had taken account of my free labour in planting the seed for him. "Here, there was not much by way of soil, so, whilst the seeds did quickly sprout and grow, when the sun fell on the ground, because the soil was not deep, the plants were scorched, and they withered, for they had but little by the way of roots." These were farming folk, I knew they would be picturing the things that I was describing; the birds had been a nice touch, but I did not think I would need to create further imagery.

Now, I was in a shaded corner of the field; briars, thistles, and brambles still held sway here. I made more of a drama of my seed-flinging here, tossing it upward, so that it glistened somewhat in the morning sunshine. "But, some of the seeds fell amongst thistles and choking weeds which sprang up more quickly, strangling the life out of the newly growing wheat."

For the final part of my dramatisation, I strode into the open part of the field; it was a wide belt between those who were seated on the ground and my disciples and me. Here, I cast many handfuls upon the soil, saying: "But other seed fell upon the good soil. Here it quickly sprouted, throwing down strong roots; growing in the open, it had the space that it needed to thrive. Each single seed yielded a plant with multiple ears; so each seed had produced a crop which multiplied its number thirty times; sixty times; even a hundred times!

"The seed is a wonderful thing; like the tiny mustard seed, from which a huge shrub grows, one seed of wheat makes several stalks of wheat, and those stalks hold bountiful heads, and those heads hold multiple seeds. Here, count the seeds." I passed the sack with the remaining seeds – there were still many seeds in the sack – to a bewildered man at the front of the crowd. He did not know if he really was expected to truly count them or not; so, he just carried on staring at me, mouth somewhat agape. I finished with: "So it is with yeast, too: the tiniest amount lifts a huge batch of dough. Whoever has ears, let them hear."

We sat now with the crowd, sharing bread. The dramatisation had spoken to many of them, they even understood it, somewhat! Here and there, I filled in gaps for them, providing deeper understanding. They were much like that field of grown wheat now, bending and swaying in the breeze, but now they bent towards me, not away from me. To one, I said: "Do not let the worries of this life, things like the deceitfulness of wealth and the desires for many things, come in and choke the words that you have heard this day!" To another: "Hear the words that I have spoken, accept them, and you will blossom, producing such abundant joys, perhaps thirty, sixty, or even a hundred times more joyful!" I had sown my seeds; they had taken firm root with many!

As the crowds dispersed towards the end of the day, I announced to my disciples my intention to move to a quiet place to pray before we returned to our dwelling. They had heard me say many times that I was off to pray. They had heard me pray for them. Now they asked, "Lord, will you teach us how to pray?" They knew how to praise, even though sometimes it was without their hearts being fully in it. Some had more of a voice for singing than others, but if their hearts were in it, then their words were all as sweet to my Father's ears. They had said the words of devotion, the Shema, many times, too; some might call those prayers as well, but I knew what they wanted, to be truly able to speak *with* my Father. I sat quietly for a while, thinking how best to explain what they wanted to know. "When a child speaks, often you hear two things, the words that come from their mouths, but also the words that are on their hearts, but which they do not say. So it is with the Father: he hears the words that you say, and the words that are in your heart. So, do not fret over not having the eloquence of the most highly trained of holy men, or of the finest orators and readers of Scriptures. Speak plainly. Speak honestly. Speak out loud, or speak inside; he hears both as well.

"Perhaps it will help you if we learn together a prayer? Something that you can always start with each time, in the same way that you start each day with the Shema or the Amidah." I recalled that which I had started in the wilderness, and which I had subsequently refined, refined more, and then refined further:

"Try to learn this," I suggested. "Let us make it a part of our daily routine:

Our Father-Mother Who art above us, and within us:
Hallowed be Thy Name in tri-fold Trinity.

In Wisdom, Love and Equity, Thy Kingdom come to us all.

Thy will be done; as in Heaven so also on the Earth.

Give us, day by day, to partake of Thy Holy Bread, and the fruit of Thy Living Vine.

As Thou dost forgive us our trespasses, so may we forgive others who trespass against us.

Shower upon us Thy goodness, that to others we may show the same.

In the hour of our temptation, deliver us from the evil one.

Amen.

"It says much, in but a few words, does it not?"

We said it together several times; one or two of them struggled, so each time we prayed I simplified it further in places; later, I added a more complete ending.

NO HOME BUT THE ROCKS WHERE I LAID MY HEAD

For a long while I had ached for home. But I had been rejected in Nazareth. And that really hurt, more, in many ways, than some of that which was to occur in my future. I had been chased from that place by the religious leaders. They did not believe that Nazareth – humble Nazareth – could be the home city of their Messiah. They seemed to think that he should come from some lofty citadel and be robed in white, not some itinerant wanderer dressed in coarse robes, and with dust on his feet. So, a drifter I must be. We were fortunate now, though: after the dramatisation in the field, this town had welcomed us into their heart. We were accommodated, we were fed, we were well looked after. One of the richer landowners had given his house over to us as a meeting place; this was indeed generous, but brought with it its own problems. Outside, when the crowds gathered there was limitless room; inside, when we were constrained by the walls, with everyone trying to get in, to listen, for healing, to petition, for curiosity, then it could become truly cramped – and that is how it was this day! It was a warm day, so inside we sweltered within the confines of the room. The room itself was large, with wide windows high up in the walls. There were tapestries on both walls and floor; there had been many furnishings, but my disciples had moved those out to give us more room. Just a simple wooden chair remained. I had not wanted even that, but they insisted that I have some comfort.

The day wore on, with people quick to enter the room but very slow to leave it. So it was that we were not even able to stop to eat. My disciples had wanted to pause at the middle of the day, to eat a little, and to rest, but I refused. "No, let these people be our sustenance!" I told them. They knew me well enough by now not to argue.

Suddenly there was a commotion from outside the door. Crowded together though we were, a space opened up amongst the people. Into it shuffled a man with wild staring eyes which darted this way and that; straggly unkempt hair crowned his head and chin; some clothes hung from his wiry frame, but they left much of him exposed. He seemed to be holding a conversation with himself. There were two voices, one harsh like boulders grinding together, the other quiet, timid: "No, we do not wish to go in here!" "But it might bring me peace." "No, quiet! Take us out again!" The man shuffled from left to right, even turning somewhat, as though he performed some primitive dance. "Let's just talk?" "No, talking is for fools. Let us go and make mischief!" "Please." "No, he is in here. We know who he is. He doesn't like us. He will kill us!" The reply was timid, cowed: "Please?" "NO!" The man turned to leave.

I spoke quietly: "Wait." The figure stopped, but did not yet turn. I felt the conflict, the warring within him. This man had been possessed for so long that he lived in constant fear of his possessor. He was barely alive, but the possessor kept him from death. He liked this host, he was easy to cow, he didn't want to have to find another. This time when he spoke, the grinding of boulders was louder, seeking to grind down those around him: "We know who you are. We know where you come from. We know *whose* you are. We are leaving."

An anger broiled within me, but I suppressed it. It grieved me greatly that although these demons had no power over men still they managed to inveigle their way in. In calmer tones than I felt like using: "Yes, you may leave. But he stays here." This last part, a command. Recognising his defeat, with a shriek, the demon left him; a shimmer of black mist and he was gone. The man blinked and looked around him; for the moment he was bewildered. Matthew stepped up and drew him to a quiet corner of the room. They knew now how to handle those who had become unpossessed: take them quietly to one side, explain what had happened, and, at the same time, strengthen them to prevent the demon's return.

No sooner had this happened than another who wished to cause evil stepped out from the side of the room, but this one was a Pharisee. He was not possessed – well, not in that sense – but he wished to cast me down. "See!" he yelled. "This one who sits before you," a sneer, "on his wooden throne! He must be possessed by Beelzebub himself! Only a demon could drive out demons!" I sighed inwardly; why were they so dogmatic? What was it that they feared?

Could they not accept the changes that were coming? Of course, I knew the answer to all of those questions, and it was *no*. I called him forward, and in that same calm voice that I had used to exorcise the evil spirit, I said to him, “Tell me, friend, would Satan contend with Satan? Would I pitch demon against demon rather than against the godly? Would a demon cast out a fellow demon, or would he welcome him? Could Satan drive out Satan? When a kingdom, or even a village, is divided against itself, will it not fall? If family is divided against family, can it continue to stand?” I paused for him to speak, but he just puffed a bit, so I carried on with the parable, hoping against hope that he might have the ears to hear. “Would you enter into the house of a strong man, uninvited, unless you were certain that he was fully restrained? Then you could plunder his house!” This was all too much for the Pharisee, he exploded with: “I am no common criminal! I do not steal from another man!” “No, but you do steal faith from these people; you burden them with unnecessary regulations; you rob them of their hope!”

Stung, he left the room, muttering against me. And his departure seemed to mark, also, the end of that day’s work. The shadows were indeed growing long outside; the chill of the night had started to descend. Talking with my Father that night, it was plain that he felt we had spent long enough here and that it was time to move on to another place.

And now, a final interruption to the day: though the people still hemmed in around me (the room stifling warm (unlike the chill outside) from the press of bodies in it), Mark found his way to me. Quietly, he told me that my mother and brothers were at the door. Whilst I yearned to see them all, as it had been a good while since I had seen my family, it would have meant either trying to leave the room or adding even further to the press around me. Neither would have worked well.

"Should I let my family drive me away, drive me out, from the task that I must do?" I asked him. "Here sit my brothers and my sisters, with my mother, all are with me." I indicated those who were in the room. "Those who would seek to divide us are acting in support of the Evil One!" Some of them thought that I referred to my mother and my brothers in saying this. The prompting of people to act, to speak, can indeed be a trick of Satan's: he might whisper things that seem wise, helpful, caring, and so his words become repeated, in innocence, but to the detriment of the listener! I think that Mark misunderstood when I said this to him. Their arrival, however, did reinforce to me that it was time to move on. That evening, after the sun had set, and we had eaten a little, we grouped together at the outskirts of town. Then, I was able to see my family. Mum fussed over me: was I eating enough (she had answered no, before I could even speak)? Was I getting enough sleep (again, she answered her own question)? Was I drinking enough? She motioned for my brother to pass me a waterskin. I drank deeply; I was indeed thirsty! “Come, let us walk for a little,” I said. “It is a pleasant evening, and it is time for us to move on.” It gave me the chance to chat with my brothers, particularly James, who I had missed a lot; we were very different – although complementary – in our characters. A gibbous moon rose behind us as we walked, casting watery faint grey shadows upon the ground; those shadows lengthened at first as it rose, but then, as it slid higher, they began to shorten again. The night sky was punctured too with a billion tiny stars, all of them watching our progress.

THE SINFUL WOMAN AND THE JAR OF PERFUME

One evening, having reached our next destination, we were dining in the home of one of the Sadducees. He was hoping to learn things about me that could do me harm. I did indeed hope that he would learn from me – but learn a very different lesson. As was the way of the Sadducees, he had (in his eyes) honoured me by seating me at his table; my disciples were at a lower table, some even in another room. He probed me, asking testing questions: *What would I do if…?*; *Was it right that…?*; *If it should happen that…?*; *Which is more honourable…?*; he searched hard for the chink that would allow him to decry me, to belittle me.

As we talked and ate, there was a tumult in one of the outer rooms, a raising of outraged voices. The voices presaged the entry of a woman into our room. She was adorned with much jewellery (gifts from admirers); her clothes were highlighted with ribbons of scarlet. Several members of the household sought to detain her so that they might evict her; I saw my host give a subtle sign to them to leave her and let her enter; the ghost of a wry smile flickered across his face. So, this was his grand snare! The woman came and sat near to my feet. At first, she sat some way distant from them. For the first time in many a long year she was overcome by shyness, abashed. Briefly, our eyes met; mine poured out compassion, which hers hungrily drank in. Emboldened, she shuffled nearer. My compassion was now mingled with forgiveness; when that duopoly entered her, sank into her eyes, it was met with an outpouring of her shame; that shame manifested itself in tears as I tried to help her, to wash her clean of that shame. Her tears fell on my still dusty feet, at first streaking the dust marking them with darker lines as the tiny rivers ran along my feet. As the tears grew stronger, they soaked my feet, removing the dust entirely. Now, she was unbraiding her hair; gold and scarlet cords fell to the floor around where she knelt at my feet; they were cast off with the abandonment of all fear. Her thick tresses fell loose. She gathered those tresses together and used them to wipe the moisture from my feet; at the same time, she bent to kiss my feet.

From her cloth bag, she drew out an alabaster jar of oil, the stopper of which had been sealed in its place with clay. She now broke that seal; I detected the first waft of its sweet perfume. Now, the woman changed her position to one of kneeling in front of me. She lifted first my left foot, placing it on her skirts, and onto that foot she poured out some of the oil – a lot of the oil – and started to massage it into my foot. She poured on more oil, careless that it now started to stain her skirts. When she had finished massaging the oil into my left foot, she repeated the process with my right one, all the while taking such care and delight in administering to me.

The Sadducee could contain himself no longer: "Clearly, you do not know what sort of woman this is!" he said, unable to contain his glee. "You allow her to enter this room; you allow her sinner's hands to touch you in such a way! I say that you cannot be who you say you are, otherwise you would have known this woman for who she is!"

"Who she was." I corrected him. "But this woman has shown me far more care and hospitality than you have. When I entered your house, you did not cleanse my feet; you did not greet me with a kiss; you did not care for me. In washing me, she has washed away her own sins." For now, I did not mention that the perfume also prepared me for the grave, although I did allude to it.

"Who are you, to forgive sins?" he challenged.

"I am the Son of my Father; therefore, that authority is given to me. Will you choose to be cleansed of your sins?"

He was on the verge of telling me that he had none, but then the trapper thought he saw a snare before him (he was wrong – that is not my way) and feared that he was about to become the trapee, so instead he offered: "Three days I have welcomed you into my house. Three days have I fed you. Three days have I given you comforts."

"These things are true, but it was for your comfort that you gave them; you sought to be the one to bring me down. As Jonah, I have spent three days in the belly of your house – just as I will spend three days in my tomb before I step from it. And now, as Jonah was vomited from the belly of the sea monster, it seems that I too am ejected!" Gathering my disciples, we left that place.

It seemed that Judas, too, was annoyed by the incident. Later he told me: "We should have prevented her from breaching that jar! We might have sold that for many denarii and used the money to help the poor. But now it has been wasted and will do no one any good!" "Did it not do me good," I asked him, "preparing me for that which lies ahead, for that which will soon be here?" I knew that still they did not understand me, and that they would not until after it had come to pass.

FEEDING THE MULTITUDES

The pattern was the same in this place as it was in all the others that we had been to recently: after a time, no dwellings were big enough to contain us and all the people who sought us out, to listen, for healing, from curiosity, or to ask questions. It felt akin to the joy that a chef must experience when every table in his restaurant is filled, every day, and there are queues at the door: delighted that he is successful, that the word has spread about his food. But, boy, the challenge of feeding them all with delicious food – and all to the same standard! And so it was that we had to move on to the outskirts, finding natural amphitheatres where we might gather. In the foothills just outside the town, we did indeed find such a place.

I felt the press of them as they gathered; the babble of their voices crowded me; the Spirit that connected us all fed their inner thoughts, feelings and emotions to me. I quietened my mind, but not my heart, to them all.

They were so hungry this day for my words. They sat where they were throughout the day; not one of them left though the sun beat down upon them and they grew hotter and thirstier but not wearier. I spoke several of the parables that I had told before. Then I paused. I waited on the Spirit to lead me to the place in which those gathered most needed me. On some occasions, that was healing; on some it was further words; for some it was explanation; for still others compassion; other demands and needs there were too. On this day, their hunger was for more words – it seemed that word of my enacted parable with the sack of seeds had reached them, and they wanted more of this. But, sometimes, what they thought that they wanted was not what they actually needed. And so I just spoke more until my throat grew dry and hoarse.

And now there was amongst them a new hunger. That was the physical hunger to be fed. All day they had sat with me, and now, as the sun began its final descent from the sky, that hunger for food awoke amongst them. Peter came to me. "Lord, there must be four thousand, maybe even five thousand, here. Send them away so that they might find food to eat."

I was, as always at the end of these days, exhausted: "You feed them!" It was not an angry repost, it was more of a challenge. Peter looked blankly around him and shrugged, "We have naught but grass to give them!" At that moment, a young lad approached me; over his arm was slung a basket, covered with a cloth. "Master, I have brought food for you and your companions." He must have been around thirteen years old, but was mature beyond his years; his eyes grew wide with astonishment (and some disbelief) when I replied, "No, you have brought nourishment for all who are here." Those large saucer-like eyes blinked; he lifted the cloth to reveal five loaves and two dried fish. Overcome with an unexpected shyness, he could not voice his confusion; but in the revealing of the tiny number of victuals, he hoped that they would say for him, *Lord, there is not sufficient here*. Gathering my disciples to me, I prayed over the basket. “Father, thank you for these bountiful riches; thank you for this manna and these fruits of the sea; bless them, and bless those around us as they eat of them.”

Each loaf I broke in half. As I broke the bread, I felt a pull on my own sinews. I knew what that presaged. Each time I broke bread after that, those pains grew; it was to the extent that on occasion my first thought was to avoid breaking bread – whether it was for five thousand, or just the thirteen of us – but I knew the origin of those thoughts, knew that it was not a pain to be sidestepped. Taking the torn bread, I gave half to each of ten of the disciples; “Take. Share.” To the two remaining disciples, I gave each a fish with a similar instruction: “Take, flake, share.”

They set off in different directions, clearly expecting to feed but a handful of those sitting nearest. But each time that they broke, or flaked, it astounded them – and those around them – to see that neither the loaves, not the fishes diminished. As with Moses, when he fed the people in the wilderness (he was, in some ways I suppose, our first disciple), there was sufficient for all but without waste; the remnant, that was cleared into baskets, was taken back to the surrounding villages to feed those who had been unable to make the journey to the hillside. As the last of the light of dusk departed from the sky, so the last crumb was consumed; none remained.

As the crowds coming to see me, to listen to me, grew in the days, weeks, and months ahead, so this feeding was repeated on several occasions; each time it was mostly with bread and with fish, although on one occasion there were fig cakes too.

THE WIND AND THE WAVES

When the time came to move on again, I sent my disciples ahead of me. I wanted to spend some quiet hours with my Father. The last weeks had allowed only brief snatches between us as I had knelt before sleeping each night. Matters were now rushing towards their final conclusion; time, as it seemingly does, was speeding up towards that end of times, which was also to be a beginning of the next times.

They set off in one of the larger fishing boats, with its captain at the helm, to cross the Sea of Galilee. It was a dark night; black thunderheads obscured the moon and blanketed out the stars. As they took to the water the rains came, cold and heavy. I did not seek shelter but let the rains drench me; they were cleansing. The winds came, chilling the waters that had now soaked through my robes, raising goosebumps along my arms and causing me to shiver – but it was a focus, not a distraction. My Father and I spoke of the coming times for an hour or more. And then a sudden urgency came upon me to catch up with my disciples. I did not even wait to find a willing captain to take me out amongst the crashing waves, I just walked out onto them. I was walking on the foundations of the New Jerusalem that my Father was laying (when that day comes, the Garden will be restored, albeit that it will be a much larger Garden than before, one that will cover the whole earth; the seas – the chaotic waters – will be no more). I say this purely as a factual thing; I do not seek to explain what was still the miraculous. It is true to say that all miracles have their roots in Heaven; when Heaven finally comes, fully comes, there will be miracle after miracle – but they will no longer be called miracles, they will just be normal day-to-day life.

I let my Spirit guide me towards their boat. My eyes could see no more than the huge waves that rose and fell on all sides of me, their peaks frothed white before that white was whipped away by the wind to soak me still further. The spray of the waves competed with the rain from the skies; it came from all directions. My hair and my lips became crusted with salt; my eyes grew raw red from the irritation of the salt. Finally, I saw their boat. It was now less than a stadion away; I was glad to have caught up with them.

They saw me at around the same time, but their reaction was very different to mine: they were terrified. I heard them yelling to each other: "A ghost! A ghost walks upon the waves! The spirits are coming for us! Is it death stalking us down? What horrors does it portend?" How soon did they revert to primitive type! It was as though all they had learned in the last few years was wiped away in a moment. That was unfair of me to think that; it was their panicked minds speaking out.

I thought to reassure them, and shouted across the waves, "Fear not! It is I come to join you, as promised." Instantly they recognised my voice, and with it, they knew who it was walking towards them.

Unsurprisingly, that raised other questions amongst them. Those questions were drowned out by Peter's voice booming across the waters: "Lord! Is it really you? Yes, I can see that it is you. Lord, if you command it, then I will come to you; I will tread the waves as you do." "Let it be so. Come out to me."

He vaulted the side of the boat, but did not initially let go of the gunwale whilst he tested his feet on the water. When they did not sink below the surface, with confidence, he set off towards me. The waves battered him, challenged him, thrashed him from all sides. They distracted him; they washed the confidence from him; he started to flounder. Rapidly, I closed the distance between us. He was sinking slowly as if in quicksand rather than water. I reached out my right hand as though in greeting; we clasped forearms. "Well met, Peter! The rock now walks the waves!" It was enough. His confidence returned and he stepped up, as though from a hole.

Together we strode the waves back to the boat. Many hands helped to heft us up onto the timbers of the deck; they were clearly unsettled by the miracle that they had witnessed, and wanted us to stand on a more natural footing. They had suffered enough for this day. I raised my hands over the waves and commanded them: "Enough! Be still!" Now I lifted my head and spoke into the wind: "Cease! Blow no more!" Within moments the waves had ceased, the winds had died to a mere breeze, and the clouds had swept from the skies as though they had never existed. They drew back to reveal a bright full moon and a black sky peppered with a myriad of stars. Now they were as amazed as they had been frightened moments before: “Lord, even the wind and the waves go at your command! Every day with you produces new wonders!” This came from Matthew, though it could have come from any of them.

CONVERSATIONS AT THE WELL

A hot sun burned down; it heated the ground on which we walked and sought to prise its way through the robes covering our arms and heads, to scourge and burn our flesh. We were all weary from the heat and from a lack of hydration. During the late morning, we had arrived in Sychar. I was resting and contemplating by a well (one part of those contemplations was over a woman who I knew I was about to meet).

Having refreshed themselves at the well, my disciples had headed off into town in search of food. Despite all that they had learned, they still followed the habits of eating at certain times, of washing at certain times, even sleeping at a particular hour – especially those who had previously been fishermen. They were now grasping the concept of prolonged fasting, but, afterwards, they still returned to their regular routines.

My eyes were closed as I reflected; I felt a brief shadow pass across in front of me, a darkening of the intense light that was forcing its way through my eyelids. With other senses, I felt her hesitancy, a temptation to move on and return another time. Here was a woman in great internal pain; a pain that she had tried to hide through living adulterously, vicariously, seeking to numb the internal pain through physical pleasure. But, before she had the chance to act, with eyes still closed, I spoke: "Woman, fetch me some water to drink if you will?"

I felt her shock that I – a Jew – had spoken to her, and again that temptation to run from me. "How is it that you, of a different creed, speak to me who am but a woman?"

"Ah, If you only knew the gift of God and who I am that asks you for water, then, surely, you would have asked Him and He would have given you the true *living water*!"

Still, she could not believe that she was having this conversation, although the first shreds of hesitancy had started to fall from her: "But, sir, you have nothing with which to draw even a drop from this well – and this well is deep. So, where can you get this *living water*?"

Opening my eyes, I indicated the well: "Everyone who drinks from therein will become thirsty again. But those who consume the water of which I speak will never thirst again. Her eyes widened; the beginnings of belief. "Please," she implored, "give to me this water! Where can I find it?"

"Go, fetch your husband and return," I instructed.

Her eyes became hooded once more; her face dropped, drawing back into the shadows of her cloak, the shadows of her shame. "Sir, I have no husband."

It was time to deliver the full revelation: "No indeed, that is true. You have had five husbands, and the man with whom you are now living is indeed not your husband, so you speak a truth. But, bring him all the same!" I was about to reveal, too, the true source of her pain, but for the moment I held onto that. If she was not yet ready to release that truth, I would not force it. Later that evening as we spoke quietly together, she revealed to me that which I already knew.

Before she left, she questioned me then about our Jewish beliefs, our places of worship, our different temples. I replied, by telling her that soon the world would become the temple, and that all would worship the Spirit and the Truth; I ended by telling her that I was the one through whom all of this would happen. "You are the Christ, the Messiah," she whispered, but it was a statement, not a question. I repeated my instruction to her to go and to fetch her man. Hope of forgiveness flared in her eyes, she turned and half-ran back in the direction of Sychar, despite the beating heat of the sun. I could almost see the shame peeling from her, like so much sunburnt skin.

Soon, she did indeed return with her man. But it was not just the two of them; a whole host descended upon Jacob's Well! She had not only told her man, she had told many others in the village, who had told, also, their friends. Now they all came to see for themselves. "This is he," she said, unnecessarily. For some, her testimony was already enough; for others, when they saw, they believed; of the remainder, most believed when they heard me speak – although some returned to the village unchanged. They questioned me, and I did my best to answer, sometimes with a direct response, sometimes with a parable – these were mostly farming folk, so I spoke much of sowing and reaping.

It was during one such telling that my disciples returned; they had brought bread, grain, and some olives. "Eat," they urged. I answered them: "Do you not see the banquet before me? I have food to eat that you cannot see!" Many from the village had brought food too, for themselves and, in many cases, to share with me.

As the afternoon wore on, we sat around the well; me with my back to it, resting against it; they in semicircles, fanning out from where I sat, my disciples on either side, just behind me. We shared food, passing it amongst ourselves, Jew and Samaritan, eating of the same loaf, drinking from the same cup. I spoke more parables, telling them of the coming days; they, questioning me. I, revealing that I knew others amongst them and not just the woman; I told things that only the Father could know (of course, I knew all of them, but needed only to share concerning the few, for they believed readily).

As the sun descended, and the evening grew chill, they took us back to their village, accommodating us in one of the larger houses. Many crammed themselves into that house too, to hear more from me. It was not until the small hours that they finally turned to their rest – only to return the next morning to hear more. Three days and nights we stayed there, until the time came to move on. I left behind a changed village, but I would have been happy to leave behind just that one changed woman; a woman who finally knew her true worth.

RULES AND REGULATIONS

We had put out across the sea again. We were still several hours from the other shore; the battering of the wind and waves had caused us to make very slow progress. Fortunately, there was no rain this time. And so, for a while, we sat on the deck in quiet contemplation and discussion. I never tired of hearing the sound of the waves lapping against the timbers of a boat, even when it was very vigorous lapping as it was on this day! Once we had talked of the recent wonders, we turned to wider questions. As was often the way, Matthew asked a probing, insightful question: "Rabbi, is Moses no longer relevant? In the scrolls of Leviticus, there are prohibitions on those who have defects coming near to the Holy of Holies and those who are priests. It talks of those who are blind or lame, disfigured or deformed, those with crippled feet or hands, hunchbacks or dwarves, those with eye defects, festering or running sores, even those with damaged testicles. And yet we who are close to you are far from perfect, and you allow – indeed encourage – those with such afflictions, even leprosy, to approach you. And you touch them!"

"Firstly, as always, well done on your recollection of the scrolls! Do you not also recall that it was written into the word of the law that they could not come near, *but* it was permitted that blessing and blessed food might be taken to them. I have only reversed that – as I have reversed many things – now they come to me for blessing, as is right." This underpinned my reason for healing so that they might come near; I wanted them to come near. I went on, "It is, of course, my wish that all that want to may come near, that none are excluded. The sinners, the defiled, the physically blind (though not spiritually blind, unless they will it), the crooked (in every sense of the word), the possessed, the maimed, all are welcomed."

We talked more on this and related topics as the night passed. The seas had become calm by the time we had finished; a gentle breeze now sped us on our way. None slept, although they were weary. And so it was that we reached the end of our discussions as we reached the end of our crossing; the skies were now shaded with blue, not black, as the pre-dawn approached. We had two more stops before Jerusalem (unless a sudden calling diverted us): Bethany and Bethphage.

ENTRAPMENT!

No sooner had we entered Bethany, than the law experts (as they thought themselves) sought to engage us in debate, and through it denounce us. Forever, senior folk within the synagogue were trying to make a name for themselves, to boost their status, by fooling me, bringing me down, proving me wrong. None had so far succeeded. How could they? Every word that I spoke was the truth. They just did not want to let it through their ears. Besides, I knew the words that were on their hearts long before they emerged from their lips!

On this particular day, it was one of their experts in the law who came to me, all puffed up, fully enamoured with his own brilliance, certain in his finery that it would be he who would bring me and my "rag-tag of followers" tumbling to the ground. He thought that it was his first stone that would tumble me: "Tell me, wise one, what is the commandment that leads all others?"

Holding up one finger, deliberately, I answered him formally: "That thou shalt love the Lord thy God with all thy heart, and with all thy soul, and with all thy mind, and with all thy strength." Now, I raised a second finger. "The second is this, that thou shalt love thy neighbour as thyself. There are no other commandments greater than these."

Cupping his perfectly manicured, heavily oiled, beard between his thumb and forefinger, he asked me, "Ah, but who is my neighbour?" I saw the pit into which he was trying to push me, so I answered with a story. "Once, there was a certain traveller, a merchant, who was journeying to a particular place. As he travelled, he was set upon by robbers; they beat him, even close unto death, took all of his possessions, and left him bleeding, by the side of the road. Now, presently a priest came along the road, and he saw the man lying in the pool of blood, so he passed over to the other side of the road and walked on by. Did he act correctly?"

"Indeed, he did! This man might have been dead, so for him to draw near, even for his very shadow to touch him, would have made him unclean. Most unacceptable for a priest to be in that position."

"Presently, a Levite came along the path, heading in the opposite direction. He too passed by on the opposite side. Was he right to act in this way?"

"Indubitably! As I've said, this man might have been dead!" He stared across at me, an eyebrow raised, thinking that I had not listened the first time. So, I carried on with my tale: "And now along the road came a Samaritan. Seeing the injured merchant by the side of the road, he hurried over to him and found that he was not yet dead. So, he cleaned the blood from his wounds and bound them up. He gave him water to drink from his flask. When the man had recovered somewhat, the Samaritan helped the merchant up onto his own donkey and with great care led him to the nearby town. There, he sought out an inn, where the merchant and the Samaritan ate a meal together. Then, seeing that the merchant was tired, the Samaritan paid for two rooms, so that the merchant might have the blessed recuperating rest that is sleep. In the morning, as he was about to go on his way, the Samaritan gave the innkeeper two silver coins to cover the costs so far; he added that if there were more costs, then he would reimburse the innkeeper when he returned by this same route the following day."

Suddenly – but too late – he realised that the trapper had become the trapee as I asked my final question of him: "So, which of these proved to be the best neighbour?"

He looked around and saw the many eyes that were upon him. He knew that there was but one answer that he could give without appearing an even worse fool than he had already made himself. "It was he who came along third." He spoke with his eyes downcast, the loud braggadocio gone from his voice; he could not bring himself to say the words *the Samaritan*. I held silence for a while, letting things sink in for all of those who were nearby.

"Yes, you are correct in what you say; the third was indeed the most neighbourly. The first two did what the Torah says. To the letter. But they did not do what the Torah says in its spirit. That love should be placed above all else. They thought that they did what they did from strength, but they did not also consider their heart or their soul, nor indeed their mind. They certainly did not love their neighbour, and does not love fully encompass these four: heart, soul, mind and strength? All four are necessary for true love. A love that is strong. A love that comes from the soul. A love that cannot be separated from your heart. A love that fills your mind. Now, go and do likewise!" But I knew that he would not; he had not learned the lesson. What he had learned was that to him and his brethren, I was dangerous, that I would not be so easily trapped. I knew that he would cleave to those plotting my destruction.

SEVENTY SET OUT

It was time for my second sending, my second gifting of the Holy Spirit; the phrase *it is later than you think* had been echoing in my mind. Seventy I chose for the task: I wanted them to spread the word far and wide. In addition to the twelve, I sought out those who had also been following me from town to town – I had not called them to follow, but follow me they had. Mostly, they were of Jewish origin, but amongst them there were a few who were gentiles, some who had been born far to the south, and some born far in the north.

Seventy I sent out, men and this time women too. Seventy returned. But they returned fully changed, transformed. They had set out with doubts; they did not feel that they could do as I did. They set out with fears: would they find their way? They set out with trepidation, leaving all comforts behind. They had believed before, but now they truly believed: not only had they seen the wonders that I had performed, but they had also seen the wonders that they themselves delivered. They had felt my power – the power of the Holy Spirit – as it coursed through them each time they healed, each time they had cast out a demon. They had seen the rapt attention in the eyes of those who listened when they had preached. Yes, like me, they had those who would gainsay their words, question their authority (here, as their opponents saw it, were the uninitiated taking on the role of teacher, of rabbi; sacrilege, they thought). Some amongst the Pharisees and the teachers of the law thought that it would be simple to tie these waifs and strays (as they saw them) in knots, to fool them and to humiliate them. But the Holy Spirit gifted them with words as well as with power to heal. And so, on many occasions, the humiliator became the humiliated. They hated me more for this, they blamed me, suggesting that I had somehow used magic on these people, or on them, to tie their tongues.

The seventy spread my Word further and wider than I would have been able to. They did not yet venture overseas; that would come later, when perhaps my greatest conversion had occurred. But they did talk to those who had travelled from overseas and come to our lands. And so the first ripples, which would eventually become waves, found their way back to other lands. Word of me, and that which I did spread. If I was the pebble that started the first ripples, they were the rocks off which those ripples bounced and reflected, spreading out across the surface of the world.

Whilst they were gone, I spent much of the time in prayer and meditation; I let things quieten down around me. I spent much of the time on high peaks, as that kept me away from the towns and villages where people still sought me out for healing or for signs and wonders. On these high peaks, there were also times when I just lay back and revelled in the sights and sounds of nature, laying silently in awe of that which my Father had created. I don't know if you have ever done it, but there is much to be said for lying back on a hilltop, staring up at the blue midday skies, and then just staying there, watching those skies. Watching as slowly, slowly they turn from their paler blues to deeper and deeper blues, darkening imperceptibly all the time. And then, as the sun sets, those deep blues fade into blacks and then out come the stars; at first, just one here, one there, then their appearing speeds up, more and more burst into sight until they are as numerous as pebbles and sand on a beach. Wonderous. You really should try it some time.

But now that they were all returned, such luxuries were denied to me once more. The beginning of the end was upon me.

THE HEALING OF THE MAN WITH THE WITHERED HAND

The next day was the Sabbath. The spell of hot, dry weather continued unabated. Some of the cisterns were running dry; farmers were struggling with their crops. The dry ground meant that everything was covered in a thick film of dust as passing feet (and hooves) stirred it up into the atmosphere, where it sought, hungrily, for an inconvenient surface on which to alight. Sleeping was difficult as the nights were nearly as hot as the days, which meant that tempers were often short, and forgiveness and tolerance were in scant supply.

We had arrived at the synagogue early; I had wanted to slip into a quiet corner to listen and to meditate. But it seemed that I was to have few quiet days in the weeks ahead. Whilst the Pharisees were setting out the scrolls for the day's reading, the hubbub began; at first it was but a whisper: *See, there is Jesus. Look it is Jesus to the side! The teacher is here!* To the consternation of the Pharisees, the din grew louder; a number of those attending sidled near to our spot. At a nudge from their leader, I saw two of the Pharisees slip into the shadows to join them. They watched me. How would they bait today's trap? I wondered. I did not have to wait long to find out. A man came closer (although he did not know that he was the bait); his right hand was tucked inside his tunic. "Healer," he began; that was rare, whilst it was probably what most came to me for, they were more likely to refer to me as rabbi or teacher. "They say that you have the power to heal those who are willing to receive?" I smiled. "Yes, I have heard that too!" "May I come to you for healing on the morrow?" I did not want to disappoint the spies in the shadows, and so I replied: "Why wait? Is now not a good time? What is it that you wish?"

He hesitated, but his desire for healing overrode his reticence in asking me to do what might not be permitted on the Sabbath. "My hand has not developed

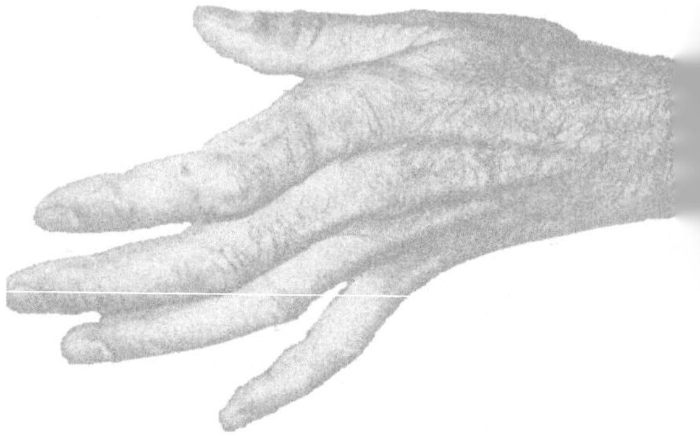

properly; it has been so since birth." I felt the gaze of the two in the shadows intensify. To the people in general I asked, "Which is more lawful on the Sabbath: to do good or to do nothing? To show compassion or to act in an evil manner? To save life or to take life?" There was muttering and murmuring, but none answered aloud. "Stand," I told the man, "and hold out your hand." He rose and hesitantly withdrew his hand from his tunic. He rarely showed his hand in public, afraid that others might assume that he, or his parents, had committed some sin and that this was the punishment. The flesh of his hand was grey, dry, leathery; it looked as though his bones were just encased in the dry skin, with no sinew or muscle beneath it. Skeletal it looked, the fingers hooked, clawlike; it resembled the foot of a bird. "The Sabbath is a day for helping others," I declared. I took his outstretched hand between my two hands, covering it briefly, letting the healing from my Spirit flow. When I withdrew my hands, he was whole.

One of the Pharisees spoke, though he remained in shadow. "This should not have been done. He has been this way all his life. Would one more day have mattered?" Anger flared within me. "It should have been done sooner, not later!" But they did not wish to confront me; word of that which had happened to others who had done so must have reached them. As well as a smouldering anger, I was sad and distressed at the same time. These were essentially good people, but they had listened to the enemy whispering in their ears. They of all people should have known his voice. But he stirred them, mostly by stoking the fires of jealousy; he fed their fears that they would lose power; he made suggestions of revenge. And it worked: I heard their whispered plots to kill me! They even put their heads together with those who had heretofore been their enemies, the Herodians, and together they whispered against me. The Pharisees had the will; the Herodians had the right.

"Teacher," the man asked, to fill the ominous silence, "have you words for us this day?" The anger had not left me (although I rejoiced at his healing), and before I had thought, the words started to flow. "You know full well that in the words that are (and in the words that are to come) there is unfairness in that which they portray. Why do the good suffer (as Job did)? Why does evil sometimes succeed?

"'Surely,' you cry, 'God should not allow this! Good should always be rewarded; evil always punished!' But look now at life; life can be unfair. Is it fair to the rabbit that the rabbit is eaten by the wolf? This should not be so for the rabbit! But is the wolf evil? Is it evil to stay alive? Would it not be equally evil if the wolf were not to eat the rabbit and so starve to his death?

"Think on this also: if good was always rewarded, then would you not all do good? Not because of that which is in your heart but because of the lust for more. And if evil was always punished, then none would sin – and yet their hearts would sin as they withheld their deed.

"Consider this man. He did a kind act and fed a starving man. When he returned home, he found that a shiny new gold piece had appeared in his clay pot. The next day, he fed two strangers, and upon returning home, he saw that two gold pieces had appeared next to the first. So, on the following day he fed six people, and six coins appeared. Day after day, week after week, month after month, year after year, this continued. The man fed thousands, and was rewarded with thousands. 'See how he feeds the poor!' the people said. 'Truly, this is a good man!'

"And then one day, the man had so much gold that it was enough to last him and his family for generations beyond count. And so he moved away, to a palace in a verdant place, and everything that he needed, that his family, and that his servants needed, he bought. They lived lives filled with pleasure.

"But in the town that he left behind, thousands starved to death, as there was no one to feed them.

"So, I ask you: was this man good, or did this man do evil?"

PETER ADMONISHED

Early the next morning, I slipped away from the house where I was lodging with Peter and three of the others. I wanted the chance to pray, to talk earnestly with my Father, to do so without interruption. In recent times, I had been surrounded by hubbub; I could hear nothing clearly. The constant needs and questions of my companions, the demands from the crowds jostling around me, pressing in, shouting to be heard. I understood that to them, all their needs were important, vital. But my human body imposed at least some limitations on that which I could achieve.

When I had set out, it was fully dark; now, the sky was lightening towards pre-dawn. Wisps of mist could be seen dancing above the ground (although the sun would soon consume these in its voracious greed), and the birds had begun their morning song. Conversing with my Father had been rewarding (as it always was); I had a clear direction. We were just about to talk over some further details, but here came Peter, striding towards me. "Lord," he said, with anger in the tone of his voice, "why have you left us to cope with the multitude? We are but twelve!"

I felt anger of my own rise, but tried to swallow it down and not pick up on the blind irony of his comment: twelve could not cope, but he expected one to do so! Communion with my Father was broken now, as his words continued to pour out: "The house is surrounded, people enter without asking, every room is filled, the streets around it are packed, it is hard to sleep, those wanting help and healing grow by the hour," he paused for breath, so I raised my hand before he could continue, saying: "Peter, my friend, it would be easy to be a busy fool! I could stay rooted to this spot and let the people come to me in their masses. But I must take the word out and spread it to others;" (my Father had just been reiterating this) "we must move on from this place."

I saw, however, that this would not be immediately possible as a small group had followed Peter and were approaching me. I did not need my spirit to tell me that the one who came first was afflicted with leprosy; the wide berth around him left by the others told me that. As he drew nearer, I could see more clearly the rags in which he was dressed. He tried to cover his disease with them (not to fool others, it seemed, his lips still proclaimed the word "unclean", but to avoid a constant reminder to himself seemed more likely), but I could see the raw and weeping flesh on the hand that clasped his ragged cloak around him, on the cheeks of the face that peered from it. He came up to me, much closer than the unwritten rules dictated. "Lord! If you are willing, make me clean!"

For that moment, my compassion poured out, overriding my Father's demand that I move on. I reached out my hand towards him, "Come nearer, I am willing." He shuffled closer, suddenly nervous; the audaciousness of his approach suddenly weighing on him. I was still seated on the dusty ground; he knelt before me pressing his face down to the ground. I realised that my face and my words to him had reflected, echoed, somewhat, the anger I felt at the interruption to my prayers, so I repeated them, more softly, "I am willing. Be clean. Go forward from this place and tell no one what has just happened. Show yourself to the rabbi, as is commanded. Make the sacrifices detailed by Moses."

Despite my words, I knew he would not. I knew he would tell others and that they would come. As though hearing my thoughts as he departed, Peter voiced: "Why should he not tell? Surely it is good to share word of your wonders?"

"My Father has been clear, Peter: we must take the word out. We must go from place to place. We must wander. I cannot put down roots; for me, there is no pillow I may return to each night. Now go, quickly but quietly, gather the others. We must move on." He made to argue with me, so before he could speak, I added: "How quickly you forget! Even after you left Egypt, saved by my Father working through Moses, miracle after miracle, sign after sign. And yet, even during that journey to freedom you rebelled! Quell your rebellion. Gather the others. We set out on the hour."

Of course, it broke my heart that I must leave behind those still in need, those with ill health, those battling demons, those with questions. But they had the choice to show their faith and follow in my wake.

I knew, too, that I must ultimately head for Jerusalem, and this particular journey's end (even though my human part cried out – somewhat – against that).

THE UNCLEAN WOMAN

If anything, in the next place the demands were greater! The fervour and passion of the crowd was palpable. They crushed in from all sides, some skirting the outskirts to approach down side streets, they all pressed towards us, towards me. In the burning heat of the day, with the added press, sweat flowed freely from my brow; I could hardly lift my arm to wipe it away. I was deeply concerned that, in the clamour to approach me, someone would stumble and be crushed by others, unable to stop themselves, pushed forward by those behind them. I called out to Simon to press ahead and bring us out of those narrow streets into the sandy plains where there would be more space to move.

As we inched forward, I felt a sudden draw on my energy. Someone had reached out through the press and touched the hem of my robe. How did I know that, with people hemming me in from all sides? It remains hard to describe; I still have not yet found the right words to describe the Spirit to your ears. Here is something that you might recognise, which maybe comes close: have you ever had that sensation when you look across a crowded room at someone and your eyes meet – you find yourselves looking at each other at the same moment – and there is a spark of something, a feeling; you know they are looking directly at you. Not just in your general direction but right at you. Well, if you do identify with that, that is somewhat akin to that which I experienced at that moment.

I tried to turn to identify the person. Hot and sweating faces ebbed and flowed. I caught the aromas of spices: cinnamon and juniper. In the haze of the heat, the faces blurred one with each other; sweat was dripping into my own eyes too, adding to the blur. It felt important for me to know who had touched me, more importantly, why. "Who touched me?" I asked. There was no response, so I asked again: "Who was it who reached out to me just now?" I asked a third time.

A woman's voice came to me from within the folds of a shawl-covered head. "It was I, Lord. Forgive me!" Within the throng there were some that recognised the voice. They pulled back from the woman, a gap now surrounded her; she was kneeling on the ground. I knew there was a story to tell. I could see on the faces of those who surrounded her that there was a part of the story that involved uncleanness. I could have sensed the story for myself, but I wanted to hear it from her lips. My tone was gentle but insistent. "Tell me, woman, what is your need?"

She looked, initially aghast, as the full realisation of her actions flashed before her eyes: she was unclean, and had done that which was not permitted – she had touched my robe. Few would see any difference between touching that and touching me. I would be ceremonially unclean. Lightly, I touched her shoulder. That I had not drawn away, that I had willingly reached out and touched her, these things told her more than any words that I might have spoken. Despite that, her eyes remained down, in deference, as she spoke: "Master. Lord. I have these last twelve years been afflicted with constant uncleanness; my bleeding never ceases. Even the vilest of cures suggested by the elders, by the medics, has made no difference; mostly they just add more pain! All my money has gone to them, but it has brought no respite."

I reached down, took her hands, and drew her to her feet. I felt her pain. Not the pain of the bleeding that had caused her such distress, and not physical pain either. Her pain came from isolation, from being completely and utterly alone. Wave upon wave of her story flooded into me in an instant. Her village had shunned her; her parents had supported her for a while, but after a year had cast her out. They told her that she brought shame on the family! Ridiculous! As she had wandered from place to place, at first seeking a cure, latterly, just seeking a place to be, she took care not to be near people. She had learned that they were not tolerant, that they did not even wish to walk on the same ground upon which she had walked. We are built for community. To be with others. We (and, yes, my human side felt this – knew this – too) are built to shake hands, to embrace, for light touches on arms as we talk, for a sympathetic hand on our shoulder when bad news comes, to sit shoulder to shoulder in the synagogue; in and of themselves, these small touches are perhaps not even noticed. But imagine them all taken away. For twelve years! Every lost contact would be like a sting, but each sting would compound the last until that pain became unbearable. And yet bear it she must. I felt the times that she had thought of throwing herself from the cliff edge, and yet something drove her to continue. It was not hope; all her hope was gone. It was faith.

“Fear not,” I responded, “your faith has cleansed you.” Cleansing tears fell from her eyes; she knew that the words that I spoke were true; the Spirit had cleansed her, inside and out. Almost inaudibly, she responded, “I believe.” And with those words, like driftwood tossed by the waves, I was swept on by the crowd. She remained, like some ancient rock, with a sea of people passing her on every side. My own eyes were wet with tears, too, from the sting of her pain, but now from the joy of new hope that had flooded her heart, her soul, her whole.

DEATH DEFEATED AGAIN

An event was about to occur that was much debated at the time, and would go on to be discussed throughout the ages. In a lesser way, similar views had been expressed around the healings that I undertook: *Why did he heal this one, but not that one?; Why did he return that one's sight and yet leave this other one sightless?;* more painfully, to me: *Why does he heal that one who he does not know and yet not those who are closer to him?* It is a hard question to answer, one very wrapped up in that which is yet to come. On the day when Heaven descends back down to earth again, when the Garden returns, death will be banished, all hurt and injury healed. That day is not yet here; only my Father knows when that day will come. So, it was not for me to heal all, even though I, of course, wanted to (as my Father does; we take no joy in hurt). Another part was the way that they framed the question, making it sound as though I chose this person to suffer and that person to become whole. That was not how it was at all; healing was in the *now*; not healing, too, was also within the *now*, but the true, full impact of acting, or indeed not acting, would only be seen in retrospect. Only my Father saw all ends. I could see many, but not all. Thus, it was often at his word that I would act (or not act). The largest numbers were those afflicted by demons; they have no place infecting you. So, it was only on very rare occasions when I would pass those by, but at the other end of the scale were the numbers that I called back from death – those were few.

We were on the road to Bethany; word had reached me that my friend Lazarus was very sick. His sisters Mary and Martha were distraught. The disciples had expected me to race off to help him, to heal him. But a great crowd was still with us on the road. My Father had work for me to do amongst them, to speak, and to heal. And so I had to put that first; there was much to do with them. So, whilst we did travel somewhat, we made very slow progress each day; a journey that would have taken only around a day, if we had walked purposefully, took over three days.

We arrived in Bethany around the middle of the morning. And here were Mary and Martha waiting for us. Their fists were clenched, and their eyes were raw from tears which still fell; anger was on their faces. They tried to make their words soft, but the grief that they felt gave them a sharp edge; that sharp edge cut into my heart. "Where were you?" "Why were you not here sooner?" "You come now, but you come too late!" "Our brother, your friend, Lazarus died three days back. He lies in his tomb now. If you had been here, that would not have been so!" Tears came to my own eyes, tears of compassion for Mary and Martha and the pain that they had been through. But then they saw the crowd that followed in our wake, sensed somewhat that which had transpired with them; something switched within Mary, faith flared anew. "And yet, Lord, even now, if you will it, there is still hope." We had been walking since before first light; truthfully, I just wanted to sit and rest a little. But I had delayed enough. "Take me to him, Mary."

"But Lord, he is in his tomb, as he has been for days!" "Still, take me there." I handed her a cloth bag and told her to bring it with her.

We set off at an oblique angle from our point of entry. This was a seldom-travelled path. It was rough, littered with sharp stones; thorns and brambles crept across it from its margins. The path led only to the village's tombs. Most of those who had followed us through the night still trailed along in our wake; indiscriminately, the thorns and brambles sought to snag cloaks and robes, to slash at unprotected feet; the smaller rocks tried to prise their way inside our sandals. The path led to the edge of a craggy mountain; like so many toes, ridges of rock stretched out and into the surrounding ground. There were many openings into the rock where tombs had been carved out by hand; those that were occupied were sealed with a single large stone, or, in some cases, a pile of smaller rocks. Those that were yet to be occupied stood open, so many hungry black mouths as though even the light did not want to enter them. It was a sombre, silent place; even the few birds of prey, that were wheeling,

optimistically, in the sky above made no sound, did not call out.

Mary and Martha came to a halt before one of the sealed tombs; unnecessarily, they pointed: "He lies within." For long moments there was silence; no one made a sound; all eyes were on me waiting to see what I would do – to see why I had brought them all to this place of burial. They wondered if I was about to offer some sort of prayer for Lazarus's soul. I gathered together my thoughts, letting my Spirit build within me. Looking to two of the men who stood near to me, I instructed them, "Roll away the stone that seals the entrance." They looked at me, horrified. A hum of fragmented sentences surrounded us, echoed off the rocks; Martha and Mary voiced them, too: "Lord, he has been within some three days!" "There will be a great stench!" "The odour of death will be overwhelming!" "Should we not leave him in his rest?"

Quietly, but with more authority, I repeated my request. The two men moved towards the entrance; they pulled the folds of their cloaks across their mouths and noses, seeking to protect themselves from the anticipated stench of rotting flesh. They put their shoulders to the stone and shoved. The stone did not budge. I signalled for two more men to join them and help; similarly drawing their cloaks across their mouths and noses, they stepped up. The four bent their backs to the task. At first, nothing happened, but then they increased their effort, and the stone started to move. I had deliberately chosen four of the strongest men for this task: they needed to see that rolling away a tomb-sealing stone was no simple one-man job. I hoped that they would remember this in the not-too-distant future.

The stone cleared the entrance, and the men hurried away to rejoin the crowd. They did not know what was about to happen, but whatever it was that was about to occur, they had decided that they did not want to be anywhere nearby.

I took one step nearer to the entrance. The silence was absolute. Long moments passed.

I raised my left arm, palm forward. Drawing a deep breath, I commanded: "Lazarus! Come out!" After a pause, I called again: "Lazarus! Lazarus! You are bidden, come forth." And then a third time: "Lazarus, step back into the sunlight!" I had no doubt of the outcome. There was a movement within, which drew a gasp from those gathered around. There were some amongst them who strained forward, wishing to see what transpired; others amongst them shrank back, their thoughts were more of fleeing. And now a figure could be seen coming towards the entrance, blinking and walking slowly as one newly awoken from an intense dream. The covering from his face had been pulled to one side; his brown eyes blinked in the sunlight, squinting against the glare. At first, the silence was absolute; no one even moved. It was as though they were models in some carefully crafted tableau, motionless. And then, as if Lazarus was the stone and the sounds of the crowd the ripples, a commotion spread. At first, it was little more than single words of exclamation, surprise, wonder, awe. Then the sound magnified as each person tried to voice that which they had seen and how they were now feeling. There were a few back-ripples of disbelief churned up by the religious leaders, but their voices were heard by only a few.

Mary and Martha gaped, blinking, first at me, then at Lazarus, and then back at me. “Come, Mary,” I said, and then, pointing at the bag that I had given her, “it is time to remove the clothes of death and dress him for this new day.” They rushed first to me, hugging me and saying sorry for their doubts, and then hurried over to Lazarus to remove his burial wrappings and dress him in the tunic from the bag. The soft hum of astonished voices continued to echo against the crags; they were incredulous, but they were filled with praise too; they gave thanks. Their hopes dashed, the birds of prey had disappeared from sight. Lazarus, with his sisters in tow, came towards me now. “Lord, thank you for what you have done for my sisters; you have answered their grief with a gift beyond price.” “It was my Father’s will that this should be so; it is an echo of the truth that death is not the end. But come, I suspect that you would relish the idea of breaking your short period of fasting!” Lazarus nodded happily at the idea, so together we headed back towards the town. In our wake came the crowds who had witnessed the events unfold, talking excitedly amongst themselves.

REPORTING MY DEATH AND MY RESURRECTION

Little more was being spoken of in Bethany than Lazarus's being raised from the dead. I decided that it would be better to let this settle before attempting any other ministry. Let them discuss the wonder; let them explore its meaning. So, I called three of the disciples to me and we headed off towards a high peak that was to the east of where we were staying. By nightfall, we had arrived at its base. Having gathered scraps of wood and fallen branches as we walked, James soon had a fire burning amidst a circle of stones that he had made. Truthfully, a fire was not really needed, as the days and nights remained warm, but I suppose it helped to keep inquisitive animals away and perhaps some of the biting insects. We ate a little bread and then spoke for a while of small things, but I soon found that the draw on my Spirit earlier in the day had exhausted me, so I stretched myself out on the ground and allowed my eyes to droop. As I drifted, I heard Peter, James, and John animatedly discussing the events of earlier that day.

I awoke before the others. To ease my cramped muscles, I walked a short way along the edge of the crags. Not far along I came to a place where there was a rocky overhang, below which a basin had formed, carved out by the waters that usually fell from the overhang in a torrent. At least, that was how it was at other times; now no water cascaded over the outcropping, and the basin was naught but a bowl of dust. The urge to bathe came upon me. In part this was in due reverence for the events that I knew were to occur this day; in part it was simply a long time since I had bathed. I saw no reason why I should not do as Moses had done (especially appropriate on this day), so I picked up a fallen, but solid, branch some three cubits in length. Taking it in both hands, I hefted it above my head and then levelled one sharp, firm strike against the overhanging rock. Instantaneously, water burst forth. Removing my outer robe, I stepped into the basin and let the water cascade over me. It was icy cold, which made it truly invigorating. I shouted aloud with joyful glee and then burst into loud, spontaneous, song:

You visit the earth and water it.

You make it very rich.

God's stream is filled with water.

You provide grain for them, just as You planned.

You drench the land's furrows.

You flatten its ploughed ground.

You soften it with showers.

You bless its crops.

You crown the year with your goodness.

The tracks made by your carts overflow with riches.

Awoken by the noise that I was making, the three disciples came to see what all the commotion was about. I was now using some of the wet sand from the basin to scrub my skin. Understandably, they looked startled to see the flowing water. "Come," I called to them, "cleanse yourselves! Today is an important day!" They took turns to step into the basin and stand under the fast-running water. Initially, Peter did not feel the need, but the other two teased him until he did. Refreshed and now fully awake, we ate a little flatbread before setting out to climb the mountain.

It was a long and fairly arduous climb, taking most of the morning, despite our early start. We could see that the summit was clear today, unencumbered by cloud, which was not as it often was, but it also fooled us into thinking that we had almost reached it, only for it to seem further away as we rounded the next bend in the path! We stopped often to draw breath, to mop the sweat from our eyes, but also to take in the stunning vistas that were revealed to us more and more as we climbed. The air was still; how we longed for a cooling breeze. As we walked up the steep slopes of the mountain, I spoke with Peter, James and John: "My death will soon come, but it will not be death; it will be birth. My gestation will be three days, and then I will be born again." They nodded. But still they did not understand.

We turned the final corner of the winding path, and there was the summit before us. Two figures stood there as though waiting to greet us – which indeed they were! They were both dressed in shimmering white, with hair and beards that were of the same hue; it was difficult to look straight at them, so bright were they in the midday light. The three disciples found it even harder to look at them than I did.

Simon-Peter turned to ask me a question, I suspect *Who are they?*, but what he saw in me silenced the words on his lips. I could feel what it was that he saw; as I drew nearer to them, my own robes were transfigured, becoming whiter with each step towards the awaiting figures; my own hair and beard began to sparkle like so much newly fallen snow. They could see that light now emanated from the three of us; in property, it was like sunlight, but in colour it was closer to moonlight. James put a restraining arm on Simon-Peter, who was following us, as one sleepwalking; the three of them came to a halt, although I carried on. “There stands Moses!” said James, to the other two. “And Elijah,” returned John. The three of them now stood, rooted to the spot; it was as though they stood on the edge of a dream – a waking dream, but a dream just the same – and as is the way with dreams, after this, memory faded quickly for James and John; it would stay with Simon-Peter for a lifetime.

I had now reached Moses and Elijah. We stood for a while smiling at each other; it was enough. Then we embraced. “We bring words and encouragement from your Father,” Moses told me. “We will talk with you of the time ahead,” added Elijah.

Angels attended us, They set out chairs of gold and ebony on which we sat; they brought forth fine victuals for us to eat; they brought forth the fruits of the finest viniculture for us to drink; they bathed our feet.

Moses put a hand on my arm, "That which awaits you makes my forty years' of wandering as nothing." Elijah nodded agreement. "I would willingly take your place if I had the strength." Those words meant so much to me; they gave me great strength. "My friends, you, more than any – except the Father – know that it must be and why it must be. It strengthens my heart and my soul, that you are here with me now; it clears my mind." Their presence really did give me great solace; they had both suffered greatly seeking to do my Father's will and keep the faith. And at opposite ends of the spectrum, too: Moses had had the weight of all Israel on his shoulders as they trailed after him – often complaining – and even he had stumbled and therefore not seen the end of his journey. Elijah had known loneliness and isolation, even long stretches of deep depression, in seeking to be the good and faithful prophet that he was. We spoke of profound and meaningful things but of lighter matters too. Moses reminded me of one of the families who had travelled with him: they had collected far more manna than they could ever have consumed in a day. The next morning, like that which others had over-collected, the manna was infested with maggots, but for this family, their entire tent was overrun with maggots crawling everywhere! They had to spend most of the next day clearing their tent, but at least they had learned their lesson. Moses told me that he was tempted to have a joke at their expense and say to them *Well, you did say that you wanted meat!* But he had decided against it.

We laughed deeply about that as we did many other things. It was a laugh of pure heartsease. In many ways, it cleansed me. That laugh washed away many troubles; it washed me internally as the chill waters had washed my outside that morning. Laughter is one of my Father's most precious gifts to you: it lifts the spirits, it heals, it cleanses, it brings joy, it bonds you one to another. The three of us cried too; tears both of sadness and of joy, as we relived moments past, and moments yet to come. Tears too are a wonderous gift to you: they wash you clean, before lifting you up. Tears and laughter, laughter and tears, they go intimately together; they mend, they bind, they uplift. Have you ever noticed that you often laugh and laugh until you are crying, and then, on other occasions, you cry and cry until finally you are able to laugh again?

The time came for me to be alone again. From nowhere, mists and clouds billowed across the surface of the summit; I knew them for what they were. As quickly as they had come, they were gone, and with them Moses and Elijah. They had returned to the place where they awaited (as so many do) the arrival of the New Jerusalem; they had been called out but for this short while. For many moments, I stood wistfully gazing after the misty clouds. Finally, I emerged from my reverie and walked across to where the three disciples still stood in their waking dream. As I drew near to them, they became more awake but still with that fuzziness of mind that is often present when you are newly awoken. Simon spoke as one talking in his sleep: "Lord, it is good that we are all together at this time, and in this place; let me make three shelters, one for each of you, that you might rest." It had not yet registered with him that only I remained. A full moon had appeared in the east. "Come my friends, let us return. Speak not of this to any other until after I have gone and then returned again."

THE RICH MAN AND LAZARUS

Looking around the room at those who sat gazing expectantly at me, my Spirit told me that there were many who needed to truly understand the nature of compassion and caring for one another. This was clear to me from the segregation that they had applied to their seating arrangements. This had not been a conscious, ordered sitting; it was simply one done from habit and deference (and for some, their feelings of superiority). I wanted to try something different from the variations that I had used previously, on the first being last; I wanted to focus on the *why* of caring for each other. But first, to befuddle their seating arrangements, I picked up my stool and moved across to the other side of the room. That caused a deal of consternation and, in some, outrage, but they could not move from the places that they had chosen, the room was too crowded. I squeezed in amongst some of the children who had taken (or been told to take) places at the edge of the room. As I sat, they scooched closer; three of them cuddled into my lower legs, two to the left, one to the right. On the right a fourth nestled her head into my lap. I smiled to myself; the Kingdom of Heaven really is made from the likes of these! It is such a shame that this innocence, this sense of oneness, this togetherness, is something that is lost as you all grow (in most cases), rather than developing further, as our original design had determined that it should.

Despite the bristling from the other side of the room, where the religious leaders sat, the room fell silent in anticipation. And so I began: “Once there was a very fine man. He dressed in the richest clothing, with many brocades and adornments; golden rings were upon his fingers; thick leather sandals were upon his feet; a finely woven sash was at his waist. He walked through the city with his head held high and his nose even higher, it seemed. Many attended him, fetching and carrying, catering for his every whim. Great store of gold had this man, which he kept in a secure room in his house. Other important men in the city vied with each other to have him attend their feasts and banquets; a special seat was reserved for him in the synagogue. This man’s name was Hashuv.

“There was also a worthless man. His clothing was made from discarded grain sacks, those with too many holes in to repair and thus of no use for storing or transporting grain. He had no shoes upon his feet; he had no purse, and even if he had, he had no belt to hang it upon or money to put into it; his only other possession was a crooked tree branch that he used to aid his walking. This man’s name was Lazarus.” I named him thus after my friend Lazarus, whose death was still on my mind – I had but recently called him back, if only for a short while.

“Now, the fine man, Hashuv, had to pass by the city gates as he returned from inspecting his many fields and vineyards. He wished to be certain that his slaves worked their hardest and did not shirk their labours or avoid their tasks when the sun grew hot in the middle of the day. In many ways, he enjoyed this time, as he could be amongst the first to see the new silks that were being brought to market, or select the finest foodstuffs and spices for those from his household to collect later; other wares and trinkets might also catch his eye. But there was another aspect of this transitory journey through the gate that he detested. There were so many filthy beggars there. These beggars were always pleading with him for money to buy food or shelter, or even for the gifting of food itself or water from the retainers who always accompanied him (they knew that they must be ready to cater for his every whim: to quench his thirst when he demanded it; to satisfy a hunger pang should it arise). Hashuv was convinced that the beggars did not spend the money given to them by others on food but on wine or on prostitutes, maybe even gambling. So, he both loved and loathed these moments at the gates.

"There was one of these beggars whom Hashuv particularly disliked and that was Lazarus (although Hashuv never could quite remember his name). Lazarus used to work for him, but he had injured himself when some of the rocks that they had been trying to clear from a grain field had tumbled on his foot, crushing the bones. So, of course, he felt that Lazarus would no longer be of any use to him crippled as he was; why should he pay him a day's wages when at best he would only be able to do a half a day's work? He did not know why Lazarus always seemed to catch his eye, for all that he tried to avoid it. And so it was on this particular day. It was a hot day – just as it is here on this day – and many of the wells and cisterns were bereft of water. Lazarus caught a hold of the corner of Hashuv's robe with his filthy fingers ('This will have to be discarded now,' Hashuv thought. 'It might be marked.') and cried out, 'Water, master, please spare me a drop of water!' Hashuv looked the other way and swept on without answering.

"The next day, the same thing happened. Lazarus grasped his robe tighter, croaking, 'Water. Please, master, I have not drunk in days. Just a small cupful to help my parched throat.' 'Don't touch me, Lalchlach, or whatever your name is; this is another robe now destined for the firepit!'"

One of the small ones looked at me. "Rabbi, why did he throw the robes away? Why did he not give them to Lazarus or one of the other poor?" "An excellent and perceptive question! Why not indeed?" I waited for this question to impact upon the room, but it did not; it was a question asked by a child, so they simply ignored it. Even the good amongst them did so, as such was their way when it came to minors. That was a lesson for them for tomorrow; for today, I did not want to lose the rhythm of the parable.

"Each day for the month, this same scene occurred: Hashuv wanting to check upon his workers; Lazarus begging for water; Hashuv passing on by (he had instructed a number of his retainers to ensure that they stood between him and the filthy one, to avoid all contact). And so too for a second month, with water becoming scarcer and Hashuv's retainers having to journey further afield to ensure that his whims were continually met.

"But then it happened that disease came to the town, striking down both rich and poor alike without discernment. Many died. And amongst the dead were both Lazarus and Hashuv. Now, Hashuv's body was placed inside a glorious tomb that he had long ago prepared for himself, whereas Lazarus's body was thrown into an unmarked pit, alongside many others who had died of this plague. The priests prayed many prayers over Hashuv in his tomb; no one prayed for Lazarus and the others who had been cast into the pit.

"However, Lazarus rose up to be embraced and welcomed by Abraham. But Hashuv was cast down into the flaming pits of Hades. Now, it is so that an abyss divides those two places; the abyss cannot be crossed, but one place may be seen from the other place. Hashuv looked up in his suffering and he saw Lazarus being comforted by Abraham and that he was held close to him. Hashuv cried out across the abyss, 'Father Abraham, I beseech you, send Lazarus across to me, that he might dip his finger in water and bring me but a drop to cool my raw throat.' Abraham replied: 'Is it not so, that in life Lazarus begged you for water, but you passed him by? Besides, this void may not be crossed, it is final.' Hashuv had no answer to this, for he knew that it was true, but he called out again: 'Then, please, send

Lazarus but for a brief time to warn my five brothers of this torment that awaits them, that they might change their path and not suffer as I do.' 'This request also I must deny. Do your brothers not have Moses and those that came after him?' 'But I am sure that they would listen to one returning from the dead!' 'If they would not listen to Moses, neither will they listen to Lazarus. Did Moses not carry the Word of Almighty God, written with His own finger, down from on high, that it should be the law of all peoples? And the tenth commandment is not the least of these; it said *You shall not covet*; does that not say that you should not be jealous of others? And therefore, show love and respect for all. Did the commandment speak only of the rich, or was it for the whole of the community? So, I will not send Lazarus, lest they despise him and heap more torment upon him.'

"So, I say to you all: care for one another, from the greatest, to the least; for that which you do will be done unto you."

TRAPS

Many had listened closely to the tale of Lazarus and Hashuv. They had understood; they followed me. But for others, they did not believe in the miracle that they spoke of, so they sought to divide the people against me; they sought to catch me with words: *You said that to covet was not the least of the commandments, so which is the greatest?* I answered them, "Did you not hear that which I spoke but only recently? I tell you, the greatest commandment is this: that you should love the Lord your God with all your heart, and all your body and all your soul and all your mind. But, you must love, also, your neighbour. If you do these two things, then the other commandments will also be kept."

The Pharisee who was speaking to me wrung his hands together, seeking to portray deference; he inclined his head, though his well-oiled hair did not move from its place. He whined as though tortured by doubt. It was such a fine act! He asked me, "Ah, but who *is* my neighbour? Should I love the tax collector who lives next door to me? Should I love the woman across the street from me who welcomes many men into her house, especially at night?" He must have rehearsed his fine words for many nights! "Tell me," I said in response, "who is it that needs a physician? Is it not the sick man? And who is it who needs nourishment for his soil? Is it the farmer with the strong and healthy crop or the one whose crop is weak and yields little? And who needs to repent? Is it not the one who sins? My door must be kept open for all those who have sinned to enter, so that their sins may be forgiven (yes, yes, I know you question my right to forgive sins, but, truly, I tell you, it was one of the seven tasks that I was given by my Father). And you, are you telling me that you are without sin? Should not my door be open to you also? Does not the physician heal all who come to him for restoration? Or should only some sins be forgiven? What way would you have it?"

He knew that he himself was now trapped. If he claimed to be sin-free, then those around him might voice misdemeanours that he had committed, even if inadvertently. But, if he admitted to sins, he would lose all face. He huffed and stormed off. I had made another enemy.

DAY ONE: TRIUMPHANT ENTRY

Six days ago, we had arrived in Bethany. For a while we had stayed at Lazarus's house, with Mary and Martha in attendance. Once more, as though foreseeing that which was to come (which I knew that they did not) my feet had been anointed with perfume. Judas was, again, also angry at the waste, as he saw it. The gap between us was now very wide; it had to be so, for him to play his part. The oiling was a second burial anointing for my feet; it also marked a further step in Judas's descent.

Still, it had not rained for weeks. The dry ground created a pall of dust that hung in the air, creating a mist-like effect; it turned the sun into a fractured, fragmented, ball of orange. The atmosphere had already been thick with the dust, but now, as we approached Passover and the crowds flocked towards Jerusalem, it grew worse. It was thrown up by the thousands of feet thronging towards Jerusalem. The dust made for a cloying atmosphere, compounded by the smells and sounds of the city: smells of animals, both their natural musk and their dung; smells of humans, the odour of their bodies in the heat; sweeter smells too, of incense and fresh fruit. It was an assault of the senses! It was hot, too; everyone sweated from their labours, from their journeying; their sweat was a magnet to the dust, leaving their skin streaked. Last night, my disciples had collected a donkey's colt and brought it to where we had spent the night. At the same time, they had reserved a room for us to share a Passover meal. I knew it was to be our last meal together; they did not know it, despite my telling them what was going to occur. We could have pressed on and entered Jerusalem by nightfall, but my entry had to be made with all due fanfare. Tensions were already high with the press of people in the city, and I was about to ratchet them up further. What had to be, had to be; I had to ensure that everyone – from the greatest to the least – would play their part.

After breaking our fast with a simple meal of bread and water, our party made ready to set out. There were twenty-two of us in all. Two of the disciples, James and John, ran on ahead; "Tell them that I am coming," I had instructed them, "that he who would save them approaches!" I knew that the word would spread quickly, and that the signs themselves would be seen without the need for explanation. We set off towards the Sheep Gate.

With the colt's rolling gate, I swung from side to side, like a fern in the wind. And now the people came carrying giant ferns – the leaves from the palm trees – waving them high above their heads. We could hear their shouts of joy and excitement. Those palm leaves served multiple purposes: they used them to wave away the flies that were everywhere; they used them to waft cool breezes, a panacea for the heat; they raised them as flags of glory. And now, as our approaching party met with their outreaching one, they cast the leaves on the path before us in an effort to curtail the rising dust; some threw their cloaks onto the path for the same purpose – well, they did not need them for protection from the cold right now! They were all shouting out in worship; they shouted out for me to save them; they glorified my name.

With an ensuing grief that dragged from me the onset of tears of sorrow, I was jolted by the realisation of how much that would change in seven days, as the Pharisees, the Sadducees, and the teachers of the law stirred them against me; they were so used to following the strict laws that they imposed upon them that it was hard for them to gainsay them, to turn over a lifetime of habit. And so, when they were told that I blasphemed, many believed it; there were also many who did not, but they were swayed by the others to remain silent. Their silence was as damning as those who spoke loudly. But I am leaping ahead, let us take each of these seven days in its turn.

I saw it in their eyes as I rode on that colt towards Jerusalem: despite my carefully considered choice of riding a colt, rather than a great warhorse, still they saw me as the next Judas "The Hammer" Macabee. Externally too, they showed it, waving those palm branches like war banners and throwing them on the path before me.

We crested the ridge to begin the decent down towards Jerusalem. The city assailed my senses with its glory and majesty and, alongside that, its corruption and wickedness, buried just beneath the veneer of the surface. I wanted, desperately wanted, to cut out that rot, remove that cancer of corruption from it, to make it clean and whole again. But I knew that it would not be so. I could hold in the tears no longer; they flowed down my cheeks, mingling with the dust of the atmosphere, streaking my face, descending into my beard. My tears were not for myself; they were for the world. I went willingly to the alter to be sacrificed, to shed my blood for the world. I knew that the sacrifice would save some, indeed would save many over the years. I would still do that which I was heading inexorably towards if it would have saved only one. But I knew, too, that there would be so many who would not turn from their path. My tears were not for me, for what many might feel was a futile gesture on my part; they were for all those of you from whom I would be unable to draw back the veil of deceit that covers your eyes and stops you from seeing the truth, from unstopping your ears so that you hear. For some, that veil was self-imposed – for those I had compassion but perhaps less sympathy – for others, the veil was imposed upon them; those who followed the dictate of the Sanhedrin without questioning.

The human part of me rebelled against this future; for many nights my Father and I had talked of it. “Is it necessary for me to drink this cup?” I had asked. “I would willingly lay down my life to save them all. But we know that that will not be so.” He had replied: “We must give them that hope for the future. That opportunity to turn and change their path. I know the price that you – we – must pay is high (so, so, high); but, we know, also, how much we love them. That we must do whatever we must for our children. What parent could do otherwise?"

A passage came to me from the Scroll of Exodus:

And the Lord passed by before him, and proclaimed, The Lord, The Lord God, merciful and gracious, longsuffering, and abundant in goodness and truth, Keeping mercy for thousands, forgiving iniquity and transgression and sin, and that will by no means clear the guilty; visiting the iniquity of the fathers upon the children, and upon the children's children, unto the third and to the fourth generation.

It brought back to me a debate that Simon-Peter and I had had three or four days ago: "How can he be both," he asked, talking about this same passage, "benevolent on the one hand and yet punishing generations not yet even born?" I had replied, "What if there were only the final verses? How would you see Him then? Only badly? Living in fear; doing what we do through fear, not through understanding?

"He gives you free will; you choose what to do with that free will. Think of the parents who you know; think of the ones who never admonish their children. Does that not spoil the child? When that child grows up and has children and does not admonish them either, then that transgression is magnified.

"The good parent forgives a child who transgresses, but becomes sterner if that child continues to transgress in the same way again and again. Oft the child repeats the sins of the father! Now, think of the parent who only admonishes, who shows no love, no compassion; does their child learn?"

Once again, I saw the beginnings of understanding in his eyes – perhaps because Simon-Peter himself was often quick to anger, he grasped it sooner than some of the other learnings.

And so we entered that great city, amid the raucous fanfare, the press of people all around us; and, on their periphery, spying eyes eager to see how I might be brought down.

DAY TWO: FURY IN MY FATHER'S HOUSE

The next day, I went to the Temple. If the hubbub of entry had assaulted the senses, the sights and sounds (and smells) before me did even more so. My Father's House should be a respectful place, a place of reverence; the only loudness should come from songs of praise. But that was not how it was. Here before me was the chaos sea, as if the work of my Father on the third day had been undone. An ocean of people eddied before me; here and there animals took the role of the fish, the religious leaders took on the mantle of the serpents.

The chaos came too from all the trading which was occurring. The first wave of stalls housed the money lenders; they took in the currencies (at very poor rates) and exchanged them for the Temple shekel. The next wave were those selling sacrificial animals (at equally extortionate prices); so also were there waves of sellers of all kinds of other wares, of jewellery, of clothing, of herbs and spices; they ensured that not one single Temple shekel ever made it out of the Temple.

After the sights and the sounds there was a third sensory assault, which was the aroma; the dung of the sacrificial animals, the odour of all those bodies – human and animal – the stench of animal fear was magnified by the searing heat of the sun.

I had entered the Temple ahead of my disciples; I did not want them with me at this time; I did not want them to prevent that which was about to occur. I knew beforehand that the scene that I was now witnessing would raise a wrath within me, but seeing it all now before me angered me more than I could ever have believed possible. My eyes hurt from the scene before me; my ears hurt from the sheer volume created by the thronging masses (and also from the things that were being spoken of – there was no reverence). My nose wrinkled, wanting to blot out the smells that tried to make their way inside my lungs; my heart was breaking – in agony – from that assault. For long moments I stood there, my face red with fury, my knuckles white around the handle and butt knot of the whip that I had brought from my lodgings.

And then that which broiled within me could no longer be contained, as though I was momentarily Leviathan myself – or, perhaps, Leviathan's tamer – I strode out into those chaos waters. I came to the first table, upon it were many baskets, each for a different currency. I upended it, lengthways, sending coins spinning in all directions. The guards who stood nearby (but who had never witnessed such a thing before – nothing more than petty filching had they ever witnessed) were slow to react; when they made to come towards me to apprehend me, their path was blocked by the many who scrabbled to pick up the fallen coins. A second and third table full of coins I toppled; like shoals of hungry fish, those present dived down to grasp at the coins.

An animal pen was before me now, tended by three young men. They had seen what I had just done, but were uncertain what to do: should they block my path? should they tackle me? should they summon legionaries? I saw doubt and fear in their eyes, but I saw wonder too. For the first time, I cracked my whip; that decided it for them, fear won out and they fled. My whip snaked out again, coiling around the upper bar of the gate. With a yank, the gate and part of the fencing tore free; sheep and goats scattered in every direction. Next to the pen stood a substantial aviary – a temporary prison – filled with cages containing pigeons, doves, sparrows, and more; similarly filled cages hung from the awning above the table too. "Why is this here?" I raged. "This is a place of worship, not for the sale of chattels! Your presence is an obscenity! All the sacrifices that you hold here would not be enough to atone for that which you do!" I swept the cages to the ground with the thicker end of my whip; some shattered, with others the cage doors burst open. Now the air was filled with birds flying in all directions; loose feathers fluttered down here and there; the birds squawked loudly, raucously, the cacophony was the antithesis of songs of worship and praise; they excreted in their fear.

More tables I overturned, more pens I wrenched open, more cages I shattered; and now, that chaos created its own chaos. Some ran towards the gates to avoid the brouhaha; others ran forward to grasp for coins or freed animals and birds. My whip rang out again and again, cracking like thunder above the waves.

As I stormed and raged further into the Temple grounds, slowly a silence fell. Heading towards me at an oblique angle came a mixed throng of Pharisees, Scribes, upholders of the law, and Roman legionaries. They had been alerted and came now to see what might be salvaged – my actions would affect both the Roman's and the Temple's coffers. My disciples had been looking for me and guessed that I might be the cause of the commotion; they now approached from the opposite direction. A wide circle had opened up around me. The group of officials arrived at its edge but came to a sudden halt; they were suddenly unsure how to act, what they should now do. If they arrested me, would it spark a riot? The last of the birds and livestock had fled and now a true silence fell. The officials nudged and whispered to each other. The Pharisees urged the Romans to act; the Romans were less sure. Suddenly, a lone voice pierced the silence; from somewhere in the crowd it rang out: "Hosannah! Hosannah! Blessed Son of David!" The shout was taken up by others. The resolve of the officials wavered, fearing for a loss of favour from the crowd. I glared at them: "Are you the keepers of my Father's House, or are you the worms and the vipers who have invaded it? This should be a place of purity and devotion, but you have turned it into a haunt of thieves, robbers, prostitutes, and vagabonds! You encourage the veneration of money; you have made it your idol. You stand there in your fine robes, outwardly respectable and pious, but inside, your hearts are stone; your hearts are black; your hearts are greedy. You desecrate commandments one to three!" My words angered them still further, but their doubt grew too. Some of the younger amongst them wanted to challenge me, but the elders were more cautious; they wanted to plot secret ruin upon me, away from the crowds.

The impasse was broken by my disciples. Simon had now broken through the crowds. "Come, Lord, I think we should leave this place." He put an arm around my shoulders and urged me towards the place where the other disciples stood. At his touch, my anger dissipated, and I let them lead me from that place. But I had lit the fuse. A meeting of the religious leaders had been called, hastily scheduled as they exited the Temple in the opposite direction. Now they would stop at nothing.

That night I spoke again with my Father. I should probably have told you this earlier, but when I say *speaking with my Father*, it's not like a two-way conversation over a glass of wine. Well, it is two way, but my Father speaks with more than just words. It is also more than just emotions, although they play an important part. Picture communication that involves the mouth, and the eyes, and the nose: speaking, seeing, smelling. Then add to that touch and taste, a potpourri of words, sounds, and music, throw in your senses, and emotions, and you will start to get close to it. Of course, some of you will understand this well, as you have heard from my Father too.

Anyway, this night I was fretting – in a very human way – about my outburst in the Temple. Had it tarnished me? Had I sinned in my rage? Whilst I had not struck or hurt anyone, in the furore that I had created someone might have been injured. *Father*, I asked, *have I brought our plans to ruin? Have I marked myself? I was just so consumed by what they had done to that special place!* I felt his hand upon my shoulder. *My Son, anyone who has a heart can know love. And anyone who knows love will also know anger, rage (and many other emotions besides: compassion, fear, perhaps jealousy, and more). Remember when I raged at Moses, remember the golden calf, remember Sodom and Gomorrah and also when I flooded the land – indeed the world? Any parent will have anger when their child goes astray, or comes close to danger. The sin is to let that anger be anything more than fleeting; to let that anger fester is a sin, so too, to hold a grudge. To experience one emotion – wonder, joy, love, hope, and so on – is to understand that each has an opposite; one cannot exist without the other, as it adds context, a framework, depth. So, no, my Son, you remain without blemish; that which must be, may still be.*

The human within me was still not quite convinced. Figuratively, my Father sat me upon his knee and explained himself further. I will never forget His response, as He told me what, in so many ways, I already knew as He made sense of my whirling emotions: *My son, there is no sin in feeling emotions; you know that it was one of our gifts to man. The ability to love, to feel compassion, to feel joy, to experience wonder; all those things we gave them. But for those things to have meaning, we had no choice but to give also their opposite: hate and selfishness, sadness and indifference. It is not the emotions that are wrong, it is what we do with them. Yes, you allowed your emotions to show, you expressed your feelings, but you did not do it to hurt others. Think again of the opposites: can you think of some aspects of love, for example, where to manifest those, or act upon them, might be to sin*?

Elements of my rage still lingered within me, perhaps rather the shame of that rage. At first, I could not see what He was saying: how could there be any sin in love? There was a blindness upon me, but then, as I felt His hand gentle upon my shoulder, the last vestiges of my rage left me; the curtain was drawn aside, and I saw. *Yes, my Father, I see it now. It is right to love your sister, your mother; but it is not right to manifest that love in the same way that you show love to your wife*. Then, after further moments of reflection, I added: *To notice another woman who is not your wife is not wrong; but it is wrong to let those thoughts grow, to become sin even within your own heart.*

I felt His blessing flood through His fingertips and into me, my body tingled, shook somewhat, cleansing tears now fell from my eyes. We shared so much, my Father and I, had done so much together, yet still I looked up to him as a true Father, enraptured by his wisdom. *Forgive me, Father. I do*, He replied, *and forgive me that I have piled all these pressures and demands upon you; you know too well, now, the human conflict. Yet I remain proud, truly proud, of how you have trodden that path, how you have shown true balance in all its ways.*

For this is one of the enemy's greatest delights: casting a veil over the eyes of people so that they fail to see the work of the good man (or woman). The good man will see a task that needs doing and just get on with it, not for their own glory, just because it needs doing. And because the good man is not boastful and does not cry out "Look, see the good work that I have done!", this makes the enemy's work much easier. And, because the boastful one will cry out, "Look! See what I have done! See how I have helped you!", the veil will become all the thicker.

I could see it more clearly now as I imagine you can too. You will have good people all around you. At work. In your church. In shops and cafés. Maybe even in your family. Do you see them? Do you ask yourself "Who did this thing?" "Who performed this act of kindness?" Watch for the person who masks their hurt, not wanting to burden you with it.

I could see how the blindness starts when you are but small; your mothers and fathers do many things for you. They do it because they love you. They do not do it for your thanks. But, on the occasions when you do see through that veil and say: "Thank you for that delicious meal" or "Thank you for the clean linen on my bed" or "Thank you for noticing that I had had a bad day and hugging me", you will see how their hearts will swell – well, actually, you will not see, but trust me, it will be so.

So it is with my Father: he does many things because he loves you.

DAY TWO: TORN TO THE GROUND

Contemplating that conversation with my Father, I was walking the streets of Jerusalem, heedless of the direction in which I was heading. All the streets were crowded with those here for the festival, so for one careless of where he walked, it was easiest to just be swept along with the flow of the people. Had I been thinking of where to walk, I might have avoided the street leading to one of the synagogues that surrounded the main temple; but the first thing that I knew, which brought me back to my location, was when I heard one of the Pharisees (he was thin and bony, as though the sun had dried him like a piece of fruit) cry out: "There he is! The one who caused such desecration in the Temple. The one who caused so much damage! How could he treat our sacred place in that way!" Another pointed a flabby finger at me and spoke to me directly; he almost spat the words, and indeed there was spittle on his lips: "Is it your aim to throw down our sacred place, you worshipper of demons? How dare you act in such a way in the Lord's place?" My anger nearly returned with full force, but, for now, that was spent; I retained my strength for the trials to come. "I might ask you that same question: how dare *you* treat my Father's House in the way that *you* do?" The thin bony one was quick to respond, "And, by what right did you do the things that you did? The wilful vandalism, the scattering of the Temple's money? Is there any sign that you can you show us to prove by what authority you did those things?" "The sign that you will see I declare is this: tear down this temple, and in three days I will rebuild it." He laughed harshly, "What mad man are you? That temple took forty-six years to build, and you will do it in three days!" He had not noticed that I had indicated myself whilst I had been speaking.

"The temple will be demolished," I told them; "the walls will crumble to the ground. The first sign will be the tearing of the veil; the inner will become the outer. And after three days it will be rebuilt, stronger, grander, than before."

They did not know, still, that I referred to my own body. They missed entirely my meaning: I was the door of the temple, opening in welcome; I was the cornerstone and the keystone too: I held the shape of the future. My body, and the cross, would replace the grandest of temples. After the day, which would soon be here, the church, the temple, would be any place where three or more met – or even where one earnestly prayed. My body would be the roof and the walls; my spirit would be the lights within; my heart the altar. But the likes of these would not know it; they would deny it even if they saw it. I shook the dust off my feet and walked on.

DAY THREE: OF FIGS AND OLIVES

I wanted to leave the crowds behind for a while. They had all but stopped coming to me for healing, but now, instead, they looked for me to lead the revolt, the revolution, that would topple Rome. They did not say it to me, but I knew their thoughts. So it was that I went with my disciples towards the Mount of Olives; there was still so much that I wanted them to understand, and so little time remained. The path was dry and dusty; coarse sand inveigled its way into our sandals, and the finer grains swirled around us seeking our eyes, our throats.

I realised that I had not eaten that morning so hasty had I been in leading us out. I turned to Thomas, who was usually the best in thinking ahead and bringing things like small parcels of food; he always distrusted that we would find refreshment where we travelled.

"Thomas, did you bring something to eat? I have a sudden hunger." He looked abashed, casting his gaze downward, "Master, I brought nothing. I am so sorry. Would you like me to return to Jerusalem and bring something back?" "No, no, please don't worry. I just have a passing hunger. And look, there is a fig tree up ahead, I'm sure that I will be able to satisfy my need from that." I could almost taste the sweetness of the figs, the slight crunch of texture as I bit into the juicy flesh; salivation came, and I lengthened my stride. But then I came to the tree and saw that it was barren, not one offspring did it have; there was no fruit, not even in the higher, out of reach, branches. My mood went from high to low. Whilst I knew it was not the tree's fault (fig season was not yet here), still I cursed it: "If you cannot bear fruit on this day, then you will not bear fruit on any day!" We passed on by, heading for a lonely plateau.

As we looked out over the spreading panorama before us, brown and dry from the prolonged drought, with only the occasional clump of green crowding around a source of water, I struggled to find the words that I wanted to share with them. There was little to be gained from repeating myself, though there was much that I wished them to understand, new words, new parables – but clear ones – were needed. And yet my mind was clouded with that which lay ahead of me. Instead, I decided that we should just pray. "My friends, please pray for me, as

I have prayed for you." At first they were silent, uncertain, nervous, not knowing what to say, or where to begin, but then Simon began, at first hesitantly, haltingly, but then with growing confidence as the Spirit fed him. The others now joined him, their prayers were clumsy, awkward, but heartfelt; they lifted me. They laid hands upon me (as they had seen me do to others). The Spirit enfolded us, enveloped us like an umbrella; I felt it, and they felt it too. For that brief while, we stood not on a dusty plateau but on the verdant footings of the New Jerusalem. Lush grasses replaced dust and stones; rich, delightful, flora surrounded us; birds sang merrily. The air itself sparkled; it was fresh, previously unbreathed, rich with oxygen; it strengthened us. Time itself paused. I had not had the chance to say any of the things that I had wanted to. But perhaps this was better; recollection of the moment itself would quickly fade from memory for them, but its impact would remain forever.

And so we returned to Jerusalem. As we passed by the fig tree, my disciples were amazed to see that its leaves had withered and in places the bark had dried and peeled. I tried to explain to them that my curse was not in anger at the tree but a demonstration against the Scribes and Pharisees: "When you see a tree resplendent with leaves, you expect that it will also bear fruit. So it is with those who are against me: the leaves are their fine robes, their positions of honour at banquets, (their own perception of) their standing in the community, their public proclamations. But beneath that fine foliage, there is nothing to offer one who has a hunger for knowledge (for they quote what they do not perceive). As a tree takes water from the rain and nourishment from the soil, they take; but where a tree gives fruit, they give nothing. And so, when the Garden returns, they will have no place in it; they will wither, as this tree has withered. But there will be a place in the Garden for he who bears even one fruit, who has done but one good deed; for the rivers and streams that will flow through that Garden will flow with the water of life, and one fruit will become many." But they did not understand. They thought that I acted in simple anger; the echoes of my rage in the Temple still rang in their ears.

DAY THREE: ON NOT BELIEVING THAT A CHANGE HAD COME

In the future, I knew that the Berean Jews would be praised for their "noble character". When Paul went and preached the gospel to them, they did not just blindly accept his words, but neither did they reject them; instead, they would receive the message with great eagerness, and examine the Scriptures daily, to see if what Paul had proclaimed was true. These chief priests and teachers of the law should equally have been eagerly looking for the Messiah. When someone came along doing messiah-like things and bringing new teaching, they should have searched the Scriptures with eyes of hope to see whether what he was saying, and doing, was in line with God's Word. So it should have been between me and those who declared themselves in authority. But it was not so. Instead, those teachers of the law, together with the chief priests, looked for a way to arrest me immediately, to have me killed, because they knew that I had spoken many parables against them. But they were afraid of the people, of losing their power, so they plotted and schemed behind closed doors.

Of course, I realised that it was so hard for them: they had lived with thousands of years of history proclaiming that a thing was going to happen; why would they expect it to happen in their time! They had spent so long saying "when the Messiah comes" that it was so hard to suddenly start saying "now that the Messiah is here"! In part, they were trying to protect their own position, their exalted status, but it was also true that they had become so used to the repetition, of acting by rote, that their minds were closed, not open.

We stood, now, near to the house of one who was recently widowed. She and her husband had had only one son; he had died tragically whilst working for a landowner some years before. It was not the landowner's fault; it was just one of those accidents that happen. Indeed, the landowner had been very good to the grieving couple, giving them money and other gifts. Whilst he was blameless, his heart was good and he cared for all those who worked for him. But he had sold up and moved on some years ago now.

Outside her house a rabbi now stood, fingering the rich brocade of his tunic. He cried aloud in lament, "Lord, bless this poor woman in her troubles! Watch over her and keep her safe. Provide for her I pray!" I saw some of my disciples nodding approvingly; they saw only that which was happening in the now – I was compelled to tell them the full story, none too quietly so that those around us would hear too, I proclaimed: "Oh, the duplicity of those who cry public lament but privately rub their hands together in glee! Not three hours past, this man and his brethren stripped this house of all that was of value – for backdated rent, he claimed. Yes, he will now offer this woman a roof under which to sleep, but he takes her in only as the lowliest of his servants. He will work her hard, with no compassion.

“Oh, how he, and his like, glory in their many tassels and the fineness of the cloth that makes their robes! Oh! How they all head for the places of highest honour in the Temple! Oh! How they all seat themselves at the topmost table at weddings and banquets! Oh! How they give loudly their coin at the Temple; coin which they have but recently taken on some pretext or other from those that they should consider as brothers and sisters! They take! They hoard (both wealth and praise!)! They strut! For them the new temple, when it comes, will be closed. They will sit on its front steps begging for crumbs, which none will give them, begging for entry to the Garden, but no entry will be given, as they gave nothing in this life. There are gates, but those gates will be permanently closed.”

I saw now a fuller understanding in the eyes of my disciples; they saw the rabbi standing next to a withered fig tree. I knew, too, that I had taken another step towards sealing my fate. Their plotting would grow more intense.

I had just finished telling them (again) the story of Salannia, how she had told her father that she loved him as much as salt. It was one of my many parables that they would not write down, and yet it would be passed down verbally through the years to reappear later in the works of others. This telling created another thought in my mind, which I wanted to share with them. "Let me tell you about the scrolls of scripture that are and the scrolls that are to come." I saw that familiar look of blankness draw across their faces. "Indeed," I continued, "for some among you will write great works, which will last for ever." Now, most of them laughed. But I had sown a seed.

"Let me continue with thoughts of food. Consider the Greek dish of orange-roasted lamb; for some, they will be told that it tastes delicious. And for them, that will be enough; they will believe it, even though they have not tasted it. Still others will eat orange-roasted lamb, and they will agree that it does indeed taste delicious. So it is with the Pharisees: they know of its delicious taste and tell others of it. But they have no knowledge, no true knowledge, of that which makes it delicious.

"Still others will want to know how it is made – the blends of herbs and spices, whether orange is the only citrus fruit used, the amount of salt to add to make it just right." I saw that I had the attention of the women, some of the men too, especially Matthew who had often cooked for himself as he lived his previous solitary life, shunned by Jews and with no real friends amongst the Romans either. "For some that knowledge will be enough. But still others will wish to know why those herbs work but other herbs do not. Or why two types of the same herb will taste different and give a slightly different result. Or perhaps why the salt of the sea is different from the salt of the land.

"So must it be with the scrolls. You can know of them. You can know them. Or you can truly understand them. It takes time and practice, just like our recipe: the first time you make it, it will not be as good as the one hundredth time, even though the ingredients are the same, and the way that you make it is also the same.

"So, do not limit yourself to just knowing the story as a whole. Know each part, taste each word that you put on the page; season it as you think best."

I looked around the rapt faces, catching the eyes of four of them in particular.

DAY FOUR: THE BEGINNING OF THE END (OR THE BEGINNING OF THE NEW BEGINNING)

Those who would persecute me were sore afraid of taking me down in front of a crowd, of arresting me on some pretext or other. They feared that that peaceful, rapt crowd would turn to a howling angry mob – with their anger directed at them. They were probably right to fear that. So, their machinations needed, firstly, to take me in from somewhere quiet, with few around me; secondly, their plots worked around how they might incite that mob anger – but incite it against me! But how might they achieve these things when they could not know where I would be at any one moment, and who – and how many – would be with me?

Now it happened that when we allocated rooms for each of us to stay in, by lot, Judas was given a room to himself. And in that room many evil thoughts from the enemy gnawed at his mind. He remembered jars of perfume wasted; he remembered times when I had not taken his advice; he remembered what he saw as opportunities wasted. He believed in my ministry but became convinced that I was hindering it, trying to do too much good. Without that, he became convinced, the word would spread more quickly. He drank wine as he brooded. And he drank one cup too many.

Also in the lodgings where we were staying, several Pharisees were housed too, although quite separately from us. Returning from relieving himself, Judas took a wrong turn and burst into quite the wrong room.

Imagine the Pharisee's surprise when the door of the room opened and in walked one who he immediately recognised as one of my followers. Already in the room were three of his fellow Pharisees and four of the Sadducees. They were gathered to explore the ways in which they might bring about my downfall.

Enter my poor friend Judas. In many ways, it was his wide-eyed innocence that led to his downfall; that, and the last vestiges of a previous greed, and the whispering of the evil one. The wine that he had consumed would not have helped either. This was not a meeting that he had planned for; he had, however, thought in his room about seeking out such a meeting. His intention for that encounter was not one of betrayal (at least, so he convinced himself). I think he had some hope to arrange safe passage for us to another place. But he was not prepared for their subterfuge, an art in which they were most experienced! Slowly, slowly, as the talking went on, they twisted things, declaring that they would "pretend" to arrest me; then Judas and the other disciples would flee the town, with the promise of my release to be reunited with them and for us all to move on. Satan's whispering in Judas's ears that this was indeed wise council sealed my fate, as did the bag of silver coins that they placed on the table (Judas thought he could do many good things with that payment; it would make up, somewhat, for the wasted perfume). It was agreed. He would alert them as soon as I was in a secluded space. He did not know that it would be the very next day.

I still rejoice in the role that Satan played as these last days played out; without his words – evil though they were – the outcome might have been different and the sacrifice not have been made. He played that key role in my fate and, with it, sealed his own fate! Delicious irony!

Other betrayals there were, too, on that day. They talked behind closed doors and sealed windows, thinking that I would not hear them. They plotted to use the hold that they had over the people: a people who were just so, so used to doing as they were told for fear of eternal torment. They went quietly calling on houses; they visited individuals; they caught those who wandered the streets alone; anywhere where they might be browbeaten, intimidated, compelled; places where they were away from their peers.

They whispered, “We are not asking you to speak against him, just to be silent and let others speak. That way you will commit no sin, whether he is truly who he says he is, or if he is not. If he is who he says he is, then surely he would be protected, would he not? And if he is not, then you would not have perjured yourself.” These words seemed wise to many. To the weaker-willed amongst them they urged: “Speak against him; stir up unrest, as he is failing to do; debunk his claims; say that he is in league with the devil; cast doubts!”

To all, they added: “It would break our hearts if we felt compelled to bar you from the synagogue, to cast you out. But there are some who say that supporting him makes you unclean.” They cast doubts, they cast fear, they used every wile at their disposal in an effort to maintain their positions of power.

DAY FIVE: THE LAST MEAL

Last night, the disciples had asked me where we would celebrate the Passover; still they looked to me for every decision. "Peter, John, you see that man there drawing water," I indicated the well near where we were gathered. "Follow him. He will lead you to the place. Then tell the owner that the teacher begs the use of his upper room." All this day, seven of them had helped the owner in cleaning and preparing the room. Now we all gathered together in that chamber, the thirteen of us.

A sumptuous table was laid before us. There was fish to remind them of earlier and simpler times, to mark how much their lives had changed. It had been steamed with anise and coriander. There was a salad of wheat grains, herbs, and dried grapes, a stew of gourds, some roasted partridges and, by tradition, quail too. There were three types of unleavened bread, fresh and dried fruits (figs, pomegranates, melons, grapes, lemons crusted with a sugar syrup, olives, dates, and sweet apples). There were nuts (pistachios and almonds), alongside cholent and charoset, and of course, there was the centrepiece of roasted lamb. There were also the symbolic accompaniments: the bitter herbs, the salt, those slivers of quail; alongside these the table was decorated with hyssop, both fresh and dried, its blue flowers giving colour, its leaves a minty fragrance to the room.

In front of each of us, a single candle stood proud in its holder; they lit up each of our faces with an orange glow; they cast flickering shadows, making it hard to see much of the room itself, just the thirteen faces, and the delicious foods laid out on the table. Each candle represented the Lord's Flame, the one that had led Moses and his people, consistently and true, through the wilderness for forty years. But now each of them had their own individual flame, symbolising specific guidance for that individual in the room; each had their own personal journey ahead (even though, at times, they might get lost, might stray from the path laid out before them); each would be visited by a flame again, in the weeks ahead.

To drink, naturally, there was wine (by tradition, we would drink four glasses, each with its own separate meaning: deliverance, freedom, redemption and liberation), rich goat's milk sweetened with honey (to recall the destination to which those initial steps away from our Egyptian oppressors, that we had taken all those years ago, following the redemptive Passover, would eventually lead us); some of the fruits had also been made into juices. It was indeed a veritable feast, as it should be, but I also wanted this very evening to be etched in their minds for years to come. I knew that this was to be our last supper together; I had told them this in hints and also directly, but they had not truly heard or understood.

Together we lifted our voices in praise; it was spontaneous, unplanned. They must have heard us from the other side of the street, as the words seemed to catch, like flame, and spread from house to house. Soon it seemed as though the whole of Jerusalem was singing.

Praise ye the Lord. Praise,

O ye servants of the Lord, praise the name of the Lord.

Blessed be the name of the Lord from this time forth and for evermore.

From the rising of the sun unto the going down of the same the Lord's name is to be praised.

The Lord is high above all nations,

and his glory above the heavens.

Who is like unto the Lord our God, who dwelleth on high,

Who humbleth himself to behold the things that are in heaven, and in the earth!

He raiseth up the poor out of the dust, and lifteth the needy out of the dunghill;

That he may set him with princes, even with the princes of his people.

He maketh the barren woman to keep house, and to be a joyful mother of children. Praise ye the Lord.

Moments later, Peter led us in a second round of praise:

When Israel went out of Egypt,

the house of Jacob

from a people of strange language;

Judah was his sanctuary,

and Israel his dominion.

The sea saw it, and fled:

Jordan was driven back.
The mountains skipped like rams,
and the little hills like lambs.
What ailed thee, O thou sea,
that thou fleddest? thou Jordan,
that thou wast driven back?
Ye mountains, that ye skipped like rams;
and ye little hills, like lambs?
Tremble, thou earth, at the presence of the Lord,
at the presence of the God of Jacob;
Which turned the rock into a standing water,
the flint into a fountain of waters.

Three more songs we would make at the end of the meal. But for now, the time had come to eat and to drink. First, we would satisfy our hunger, then we would move on to the symbolic remembrances. Voraciously, we attacked the food. It tasted as delicious as it looked.

At one end of the table, I heard a heated squabble between four of them. They were arguing who was the best disciple, and who had done the most on my behalf. I will not shame them by naming them, but I think you can guess who they were! One stated, "Well, I have definitely cured the most of blindness." Another: "Casting out demons is harder!" The other two added: "Well, I have brought the most to listen to his words!" "I have been with him since the start!" I called them to order. "You are the ones who are acting as though you are blind! Ware that a demon does not take you: the demon of pride! Watch out, lest you stumble; instead, you should remain humble!" (Perhaps all the singing had got to me!)

For a while the debate subsided, then it ignited again. At the other end of the table, I could still hear them ranking themselves, who would be Peter's second, they were asking, as though his leadership was already decided. When they talked of my going, I think they were just thinking of my going off on a journey and coming back. Well, I suppose they were right in one way! But what they were picturing was not the reality. I needed to really bring home the servant-hearted message. For a while I stared down at my feet, seeking inspiration; they were dusty from the streets and our journeying. That dust gave me my answer. I called to my host for a bowl of warmed water and a towel. When they arrived, I removed my outer garments, not to protect them, but to increase the impression of servitude. Taking the towel, I wrapped it twice around my waist, looped it through itself to leave a length loose at the front. Then I went to the first of them – Thaddeus, I think – kneeling before him, I untied his sandals, and then, one at a time, washed his feet in the bowl, drying them gently with the towel. Slowly I moved from disciple to disciple; their reactions varied from wonder, to puzzlement, to resistance (although not yet voiced), and, in one case, acceptance.

When I got to Peter, he twisted as I knew he would: "No, Lord, it should be me washing your feet! You are the greatest amongst us, yet you are acting as though you are the least!" Echoes of Cousin John from but a few years before!

"And that is how it must be, Peter." My voice was gentle, but they all leaned in on my words; they stopped grazing from the last few bowls; a hush fell. "Have I not said this many times before? Be meek! Serve others. Hold on to your servant-heart. Be the least. For in my Father's House all will be equal, bar him and his lieutenants. Each will serve each other: none will be elevated; none will be lowered."

Still reluctant, he allowed me to remove his sandals and wash his feet. Deliberately, he was not the last; three more remained as I worked my way around the table. I came to Thomas last. And then it was done.

I resumed my place at the table; one last act, in two parts, remained for me to deliver. I took one of the flat loaves from the basket. I held it up before them, "This is my body, freely given for you." I tore a piece off and ate it. I tore the remainder in half, passing it to left and right, indicating that they should do the same. "Eat this in remembrance of me." And as I tore that bread, I felt the fragility of my own sinews, the weight of that which was to come. I felt the future pulling at them, tearing them asunder. Tears came to my eyes; sweat appeared upon my brow. I felt more tearing; this time it was my flesh that tore as the jagged ends of the cat o' nine tails sank into my flesh, ripping into it, tearing ribbons from it. With trembling hands, I lifted the fourth of the wine goblets; I took a sip and then passed it to my left. "Drink this cup; it is my blood, spilled willingly for you." The cup made its way around the table from hand to hand; each drank. They knew it was a solemn moment, but they did not yet fully grasp what that moment was. As I watched the cup's slow progress, I felt a bead of sweat trickle down and onto my upper lip – it was salty, like blood. As the final disciple set that cup down upon the table, I felt the Holy Spirit slowly beginning to withdraw from me; it was necessary. I felt doubt, like Thomas, about the future. I knew fear, true fear – absolute terror – at that which was to come.

Images came now, flickering across my mind's eye as though each was summoned by the flicker of the candles in the room. Whips. Flicker. Palms. Flicker. Fists. Flicker. Sandaled feet. Flicker. Scorn. Flicker. Spittle. Flicker. Ridicule. Flicker. Denial. Flicker.

DAY FIVE: PETER'S DENIAL

"These are the final hours," I told them. "Soon, you will all desert me; you will scatter. Some of you will even deny me!" Peter roared with laughter when I told him that he would deny me. But it was a nervous laughter. He felt the truth of my statement, although with his mouth he denied it: "No, Lord, it could not be so. I will follow wherever you lead, even unto death." Some of the others gainsaid my statement too, whilst others remained silent. Two or three of the candles guttered and went out. I took that as a sign for us to take the next steps of my final journey. "Come, we will spend this last night in the Garden at Gethsemane."

I led them out into the night. The crickets chirped loudly as we made our way; in contrast, they walked mostly in silence, dwelling on that which had just occurred, perhaps on what would come next. Heady aromas of jasmine caught us here and there, together with the aromas of food as others, too, celebrated the night when they were passed over. The night itself was warm and still, the moon but a tiny sliver; the stars were myriad – an audience settling down in their seats for the final act of the play.

As we passed through the gates of Jerusalem, I repeated: “Soon we will be at Gethsemane, for solitude and prayer, spending the night there.” That was the trigger for Judas; silently he left us, slipping off into the night. The next time that I would see him, he was to become the pebble that started the landslide.

DAY FIVE: ANOTHER GARDEN

And so we came to the Garden of Gethsemane; the garden was filled mostly with olive trees, their ripening fruit adding to the rich aromas of the night. A low stone wall marked its boundaries on the side of that mountain, snaking up with the contours of the land. Within the garden there were stone outcroppings too, where the mountain's rocks had burst through the soil (or where they had given the soil no purchase to settle). The gate stood open; the landowner did not yet need to secure the area, as his crops were not yet quite ripe enough for plucking and pressing.

Whilst the night itself was bright with starlight, below the olive trees thick inky shadows cloaked the ground. That ground was covered with a carpet of soft, springy grasses and mosses, the kind that – on another day – would have made me want to kick off my sandals and walk upon it barefoot. But on this day, this evening, there was too much pressing on my mind to even think of doing that. The twelve of us entered the garden, walking up its slopes until we came to a part where the rocky outcrops were more prevalent; they would make good seats or backrests. Many of the disciples were tired, worn by the busyness of the last few days and probably, in part, picking up on my own stresses and struggles.

For a while we sat, mostly in silence; one or two of them talked quietly of inconsequential things. I said nothing; a great torment was upon me; I knew – had always known – what fate was about to fall upon me. But now it became even more real through its imminence. Was there any other way? Must it be like this? Very human thoughts and fears rattled around in my brain; I tried to still them but failed. It was time that I talked with my Father about them, in prayer: I craved his wisdom, his soothing hands. I craved, too, a last-minute reprieve.

I knew, of course, the fate that was before me. Had known it all along. Whilst I was resolute, still my human fears plagued me. Softly I called for Peter, James and John to move off with me to a quiet corner of the garden so that I might speak with my Father. "Please pray, silently, for me here," I asked. "I will move just a little further on, near to that wall, as I must speak with my Father. Please keep watch, too, so that I am not disturbed."

Leaving my friends I moved away from the warmth of the merrily burning fire (not that we needed warming in our flesh, but perhaps in our spirit we did) to a piece of stonier ground. I knelt for prayer, to talk with my Father. My friends were still learning how to pray; they tried hard to master it but found it hard to balance mind, body, and spirit, thought, word and deed. At first, I could feel the small stones digging into my lower legs; several were sharp, and I could feel them digging as though trying to pierce my skin and worm their way through to my shin bone. But slowly, as I brought everything to focus, those pains diminished, blurred, and then disappeared altogether. I opened my heart and let that inform the words which tumbled from my mouth: "Please, Lord, I beg you to come close; come quickly to help me! Hear my words as I call out to you. It is now the evening of the day; so too is it my personal evening. Let my prayer, then, be as the evening sacrifice. Let it burn like fragrant incense, that pleasing aroma rising as my offering to you; I lift up my hands in surrendered worship!

"Father, give me your grace to guard my lips from speaking that which is false. Steer me away from the temptations that now plague me. Save me from doing evil. Protect me from sinful habits and from the words of those who are experts in evil. Support me in not adopting their sinful ways!

"When one of your angels, who are ever with me, corrects me, or one of your faithful ones rebukes me, may I acknowledge it for the honour that it is: one that I cannot refuse. Make it as a healing balm, a medicine that I will swallow; may it cure me of a transgressed heart.

"When their leaders and their judges seek to condemn me on the morrow, heaping the rocks of injustice upon me, let their hearts know that my words to them were true, even if their ears deny it!

"Much will occur in the hours ahead. It will be like an earthquake that splits open the earth as though the world of hell will open its mouth to swallow my bones along with their scattered bones. Darkness approaches. But you are my Lord and my God; let me only have eyes for you! Let me enfold myself within the cloak of your love; don't leave me defenceless! Protect me! Keep me from the traps of wickedness that are set before me. Let them all stumble into their own traps! I know that I cannot escape without a scratch to my brow, without the scourging of my body, without the tearing of my sinews, without my blood flowing out onto the sandy ground!"

I was alarmed when my prayers did not receive a response from Him. There was only silence. No words came. No comforting arms around me. I felt lost, isolated, so alone. Later, I discovered that His silence was caused by His being in as much torment – perhaps more – as I was at what He was asking me to do. But, at that moment in time, it just added to the weight of the burden upon my shoulders; it became physical, pressing so hard that I went from kneeling to prostrate upon the ground. I uttered more words of prayer, but they were fragmented, disjointed; I was not thinking clearly.

When those first efforts at prayer did not work well, my mind remained distracted with other thoughts, with my fears. I edged back to rejoin Peter, James, and John to ask for their prayer – only to find them sleeping. I'm ashamed to report that that brought out an anger in me which was unjust: their fatigue was mostly down to me, and the way that I had driven us these last few days. Shame-faced, they shook off their fatigue and did indeed lay their hands on me.

Buoyed, if only a little, by their prayers, I moved off for a second attempt at prayer. I left them with the same instructions: to be vigilant, and to add their prayers to mine. I knelt again, this time on grassier, mossier turf. It was an attempt to sooth me into prayer; maybe that would work more effectively than the previous time, when I had knelt on rough ground. But it was not to be. I pleaded with my Father to take the burden from me, to lift the cup I must drink from my hands. But almost immediately, I countered that by offering complete submission to his will. Above all, I wanted, desperately wanted, to do his will; I knew my request was no more than human weakness, albeit that the burden was great. On this second occasion, I felt further vestiges of the Holy Spirit withdrawing; that was truly frightening: I had never been without it before. In my struggles of the first occasion of prayer, I had not noticed the loss, I had been too focused on my own personal fears and needs. Now I understood that it had to withdraw from me. Had the Spirit remained, I would not have truly died. And die I must, for all of you. With the power inherent in my Spirit, it had to go before my death, not after it or because of it. That is not to say I did not feel the pain of that loss; it felt like a dismemberment, a blinding, a cancer. I prayed earnestly for the strength to allow that which must be to be.

Thrice this scenario repeated, until finally, on the third attempt, my mind was clear, and I was able to have proper commune with Dad. "Father, be with me now." "I am always with you, my Son." For a long while, we communed in silent prayer, but then I spoke that which was on my mind: "We are three who are one: I am the body, you are the mind, and there is our soul, which is the Spirit. But I find my human mind splits further, tries to take its own path, is filled with a voice that is not (or does not seem to be) mine or yours. It has thoughts that are not from me, nor, I think, do they come from you. Do they come from the enemy?" "I am not sure that that is a question that is easy to answer; they may be echoes going all the way back to Adam; they may be voices from that which is yet to be." Even now, there are things that we knew, and yet did not know. We spoke more; He gave me solace and strength; He gave me comfort: one of his angels descended to me then, bringing the strength to bear me up. Tears fell from my eyes, and sweat beaded my brow. In the darkness, those beads of sweat and those tears all looked dark as though they were blood, a presentiment of that which was to come. "Father, forgive my human weaknesses and doubts; Your will prevail; give my will the strength to honour it!"

A sudden dread returned to me, filled me; a quaking fear of that which was to come. I shook as one in a fever, the tears, the sweat fell from me, making darker patches on the shadowy grass. “Father,” I prayed, one last time, “must it be this way? Is there no other? Take this cup from me, I implore you!” He did not answer, and yet I heard Him fully.

“But let it be by your will, not mine,” I said, abashed.

I had not meant that it should be passed to another. I knew it was my burden to bear, and mine alone. Yet the human part of me would have avoided it if I could.

DAY SIX: MIDNIGHT IN THE GARDEN

And so midnight came to that dark night. Without darkness, there can be no light. Without fear, there cannot be hope; without death, there cannot be life. For now, though, I am describing the darkness of the night: the moon was but a waning crescent and what little light of the sun it reflected back was diffused and broken by clouds scudding across the sky. Our fire (lit for comfort more than for warmth, as the night remained warm) had diminished to embers; their glow, too, reaching only as far as the few disciples closest to the fire. Silence descended once more in that midnight hour. We were back together, and for now all thoughts of sleep had departed. At close to one o'clock, an orangey glow could be seen making its way up the mountainside towards us. I knew that the thirteenth of us was somewhere within that glow, and that he had determined a pre-arranged signal, so that they might identify me: a kiss of betrayal. The disciples were now stirring, wondering what the approaching people wanted. They knew it would not be requests for healing at this hour. They looked to me, but I left my eyes downcast, did not meet their gaze. They would find out soon enough.

I stood as their guttering torches passed through the gate. The disciples, too, rose behind me, wary, but uncertain.

The gathering drew nearer. It was an odd mixture: temple guards, a handful of Pharisees and Sadducees, four off-duty soldiers, some general hangers-on, and, at their front and centre, Judas. They carried torches that guttered and hissed; they carried clubs and staffs; spears they had too, and some came with swords drawn. Behind me, I felt my disciples tense. Simon drew his own sword. Scant yards from us, those who came in Judas's wake halted, but he did not halt for another three or four paces until he was before me. He kissed my cheek. "Rabbi," he said. "Yes, it is me," I replied. "Were you expecting another? And thus, you do what you must; you betray everything with this kiss." Suddenly he was unsure, but it was too late for him to change direction now. The momentum was too great; nothing could stop it. As his lips had touched my cheeks, the temple guards had started to move forward. They were wary; they levelled their weapons at me. "Am I leading a rebellion?" I asked them. "Am I such a threat that you come here with swords and spears and clubs to capture me? Every day this week I have been with you, teaching in the Temple, and in the Temple courts, and yet you did not arrest me! But now you come to me in this garden, at the midnight hour, with weapons drawn!" They started to surround me. As some of them moved behind me, Simon-Peter lashed out with his sword. "Flee, Lord," he shouted. "We will hold them off. Make your escape!" His aim was off, or he had meant his stroke only as a warning: he caught the ear of one of the temple guards, and a large piece of the lobe fell to the floor. I held up my hand before things got out of hand. "Stay your weapons, Peter, all of you! This must be how it is. The Scriptures must be fulfilled; the path is set." I stooped and picked up the fallen lobe; with a brief prayer of healing, I made the guard whole again. But, as I drew my right hand back from the act of healing, one of the guards grabbed it. Another, who was to my left, grasped my other arm. The pair of them pinioned them in front of me, whilst a third lashed them together with rope.

As though marking this day as very different to those that had preceded it, storm clouds rolled in; thunder rumbled; on the horizon flashes of lightening could be seen. At first the rain was sporadic, but then, as they led me away it became persistent. With the ground being so dry, it did not at first soak in but ran in rivulets here and there. It created mini streams and deltas. It mingled with my sweat, for it was still warm. The rain did nothing to cool things down; it created a miasma around us. It soaked into our clothes. It plastered my hair to my cheeks, to my neck; our feet splashing in the rapidly forming puddles, they led me back through the gate and down the mountainside. And the disciples, bewildered, uncertain, afraid, scattered just like those raindrops; just as the rain was seeking the nooks and crannies, the gulleys and troughs, in which to settle, they themselves scattered seeking places to hide and be alone. Three of them did trail behind, in my wake, but they did not seek to come near, or to interfere with the officials again. Judas no longer led the party; he was somewhere off to their left, forgotten and fully alone. As we entered the city gates, he skulked away, overcome with remorse and guilt, wracked with shame.

DAY SIX: TRIAL & JUDGEMENT

06:00 – Before Annas, Caiaphas and Pilate

They took me first to Annas, who was Caiaphas's father-in-law. They pushed me into one of the back rooms in his extravagant dwellings. They sat me on a stool, still bound. My captors stood around me. One or two of them prodded me as though I were a side of goat that they were eyeing up in the marketplace or something that they had discovered in an outer room of their household and were not quite sure what it was. Annas stood before me, his hands clasped behind his back, his chin jutting out so that he was eyeing me along the length of his sharp nose. "So, you are he," he said, somewhat unnecessarily. "What do you have to say for yourself?" I did not feel the need to answer; I doubted he was listening. He asked several more banal questions, before: "I'm just wasting my time here when there is so much else that I need to do this day. Take him to my son-in-law."

And so they pushed and prodded me along to Caiaphas's house. They were becoming rougher, bolder in their treatment of me; the prods had become digs. He had a room set up as though it were a courtroom; at a long bench, he was seated in the centre, flanked by four elders, a scribe poised to write, and a master of proceedings. A procession of people came before them, each trying to boost their own standing, each trying to curry favour. And because of that, each tale that they told was embellished, exaggerated; they made up many fanciful things that they claimed that I had said. That might have worked well for them, but the opposite was true, as it caused their tales to contradict each other. I could see Caiaphas getting more and more frustrated as his plotting seemed to be unravelling before him; he grew hot under his collar; he became ill-tempered with the witnesses. He had just been listening to a fanciful tale in which I had flown into a room, like a demon, and cured a dozen people; none of whom (the witness claimed) had anything remotely wrong with them; they were just in my pay.

The next one came forward. "What can you tell us about this man?" Caiaphas asked. "He said that we should not pay taxes to Rome! He also said that he had the power first to destroy our temple and then to rebuild it in three days. Three days! When it took us over three decades!" The scribe made notes on his parchment. The next witness told a similar, but not identical tale: "It is true; he said that we should only give Roman coins to Rome but should keep all the other coins to ourselves. And, yes, he said that he would build a new temple, grander, more magnificent than the current one, and he said that he would do it with the help of those who follow him in three days! He claimed he was the son of our God too." For a few minutes, Caiaphas and the elders spoke quietly with each other. The scribe pointed to various places on his parchments; there were discrepancies. Caiaphas stood. “It is enough. For his blasphemies, for his false claims, for inciting people to go against Rome, we take him to Pilate so that the just sentence may be awarded!” I was yanked to my feet and, like a heifer being driven to market, pushed along behind Caiaphas and his elders to the dwellings occupied by Pilate.

Pilate was not happy to be called upon so early in the morning! Even more so, as those who were escorting me would not enter in for fear of becoming unclean and thereby being unable to celebrate the next celebratory Passover meal that day. So, we held our talks on his doorstep. I could not help but utter to Caiaphas, “Do you think that standing on the doorstep keeps you clean? Your deeds contaminate you!” He demanded my silence, causing one of his entourage to slap me on my left cheek. Caiaphas tried to be obsequious, but he didn’t quite pull it off; it came across more as wheedling: “Glorious Pilate, we bring before you one who is most deserving of the death penalty. He plots against you. He has declared himself a sovereign. He has made fantastical claims. He has committed blasphemy.” Pilate was not surprised to see me before him. Those of the Sanhedrin had spoken of me to him many times, emphasising how I made life difficult for them, and also for Pilate, as they told him that I stirred up unrest. It was this last that Pilate latched on to the most. Rome allowed its governors to do much as they would to manage those for whom they were responsible, but Rome did not like unrest. Should such words reach Rome and its Emperor, Pilate's position might be jeopardised. And he really did not want that. He liked his posting here; he lived well. On the whole, the region was not too onerous to manage. Importantly, whilst they grumbled about it, they paid their taxes fully and on time – the Sanhedrin certainly helped with that, not least as they were able to skim off some of the taxes collected to cover their "administration" as they called it.

And all that made me a thorn in his side. One that he did not know how best to deal with. He recognised that I had amassed a following, and that if he acted against me, it would not take much for them to revolt and riot. I was not a problem that he relished. But now, here I was on his doorstep; he could no longer do nothing. As Caiaphas and his seconds made further, fabricated accusations, dawn was breaking; a thin watery light crept into the sky. The rains had ceased for the moment. He concluded with "He claims to be the Son of God. He claims to be a king. He has committed blasphemy. He must die!" Pilate wanted it over with; his mind was turning somersaults trying to find a way to end the difficulty without losing face, without causing a riot (that he would be seen as responsible for), without losing the revenue that came to him through the Temple at this time. He latched on to some of my heritage that one of

Caiaphas's seconds had trotted out, and so Pilate declared: "Herod is also staying here. Take him to Herod – let him decide." Relieved to have solved the problem (as he saw it) somewhat, he turned quickly and closed his door before any could argue against him.

For several moments, my accusers stood where they were, slightly dumbfounded by this turn of events. Should they do as Pilate had instructed? Should they call him back and just demand he pass judgement? In the end, they took the path of least resistance and herded their captive off in the direction of Herod's palace. The level of prodding and poking grew; many of them now hissed insults too: "Blasphemer!" "Fake!" "Deceiver!"

07:00 – Sent to Herod

At first, Herod was equally displeased to be called upon so early. But when Caiaphas told him who the captive was that stood before him, that changed somewhat. Herod said that he was pleased to see me, as he had heard many things about me and wanted to hear them for himself. He dismissed everyone else and took me into an inner room so that just he and I could talk. He did not offer me refreshment, although he took some for himself. "So, what are you?" he asked, without any opening niceties. "Are you man, prophet, Son of God, God, usurper, rebel, king, or something else?" "You start with a big question," I replied. "Who do you say that I am?" At first, he did not answer. I looked around the room in which we were sitting; almost certainly, it was not the finest room in the house, but there were many trappings of wealth. There were fine artworks on the walls, there were carvings and statues of bronze and of marble, there were vases and ornaments, there were golden goblets, there were platters of pastries and fresh fruits. "How do you compare me to that which is in this room?" I asked. "Would a king be more splendid than that vase? Would a ruler be dressed more finely than he in that picture?"

Herod helped himself to a small pastry but did not offer me one; he took a sip from a goblet. He rewound our conversation and started again. "What is it that you wish to achieve?" "Ah that is a better question. I wish for all peoples to love one another. I wish for compassion and caring. I wish for everyone to be ready for the coming of my Father's kingdom." He latched on to this last statement: "So, you are a rebel who would bring in a new ruler?" "My Father already rules all. We all answer to him; you answer to him, even your Emperor, Tiberius Julius Caesar Augustus, answers to him – if not today, then on the day of weighing out!" That statement did not go down well with him! His face reddened with anger. He crashed his goblet down on the table. All thoughts that he had had about conversing with me and gaining responses to some of his other questions flew from his mind. I think he would have liked to strike me, but he held himself in check, instead calling for his retainers: "Take this man back to Pilate for sentencing. He insults me; he insults our glorious Emperor!" They sensed his anger and hastily removed me from the room and his presence.

As soon as the door had closed behind us, one of them struck me on the back of the head. "How dare you insult our master. He will be angry all day now, and we will all suffer!" Herod's vassals were certainly far less restrained than he was; as they took me back towards the outer door, several others struck me too. They were clear in their minds now: I was persona non grata. I had upset their master, and he would probably take his anger out on them. So, they took theirs out on me. They paused in an outer room, close to the exit. "Wait! We cannot possibly send such a fine and important man out into the streets dressed as he is!" From somewhere they found a scarlet robe and dressed me in it. One came towards me with grapes in his hand. "Eat sir," he said before striking me with his grape filled hand; juice ran down my cheek and beard and dripped onto the robe, staining it darker, a pre-emptive echo of the blood that would flow this day. Another approached me. "No, no, you should bow first to the mighty one!" he said, before bowing from the waist, and deliberately headbutting me; my head spun, and I staggered. Yet another approached me with a goblet of wine, but upended it over my head, crashing the goblet down on my head too; more dark stains appeared on the scarlet robe, but there was not yet any of my blood spilled.

When they had had their fun, they took me back to the door and those waiting outside. “Take him back to Pilate for sentencing,” they commanded. “He has insulted Herod, which means that we will have a bad day. Make him suffer too!” There was a glint in Caiaphas’s eye when he heard that; it gave him hope that he would get his way.

07:30 – Back to Pilate

Pilate was in an even worse temper when he saw that we had returned. His wife had warned him not to get involved with my sentencing; she had had a dream that it would go against him. His expectation that Herod would act gave him hope that he could avoid making a decision about me (he was not a believer in dreams, but neither did he wish to go against the word of his wife). His servants had warned him of our approach, and so he was standing just within when they knocked. The moment that Caiaphas saw him, words came tumbling from his mouth: “He has upset Herod; he has insulted your Emperor; he has spoken blasphemy, claiming to be the Son of God; he is an agitator; he is in league with the Zealots; he incites riots; he has caused you to lose taxes. He must die.” Pilate took all this in; he also took in my scarlet robe and the signs of my maltreatment. Life had just got even more difficult for him. Tersely, he ordered me brought inside. Members of the Sanhedrin were still reluctant to enter; quickly, they spoke amongst themselves in rapid debate. The temple guards were ordered to go in with me while those of the Sanhedrin went off to seek to further influence the crowd that was starting to gather in the courtyard outside Pilate's palace.

We went into one of Pilate's rooms. This room, unlike the rest of his palatial dwelling, was sparsely furnished; it was probably the servants' dining area, or similar. He just wanted to be as far away from his wife's ears at that moment as he could. For a while, he paced up and down in the room whilst I stood, surrounded by the temple guards. Finally, he wheeled and asked me: "Why are you making life difficult for yourself? And for me? You could easily have avoided this conflict with a few simple words and denials. But you continue with your ridiculous claims. I ask you again, are you the Son of God?" Before I even had the chance to draw breath, one of the guards struck me on the cheek. "You will answer when you are asked a question! You were asked if you were the Son of God!" I looked at Pilate and replied quietly, "You say that I am." It was tantamount to saying yes. It sealed my fate (although, of course, that fate was already sealed). Pilate needed some thinking time; he needed to balance out the demands of wife, Sanhedrin, Rome, and his own. Above all else, he needed to ensure he kept his position. "Take him to the holding room – teach him some manners whilst I determine the best course of action."

The temple guards and some of Pilate's own servants led me down to a lower room; a room with only a few windows, high up in the walls. The room was dark despite oil lamps which guttered and flickered; there was a slight smell of damp and other less pleasant smells. It seemed that my escort were keen for some sport, to do as Pilate had suggested and "teach me some manners", for, no sooner than we were in the room, one struck me from behind; he laughed and said to me, "So then, prophesy: who hit you?" I stood where I was, near the centre of the room; they circled around me, feeling that they were the cats who had cornered a mouse. Another struck me from behind, repeating the same question. From somewhere they had found sticks with which they started to beat me. "Wait," one of them called. "We do not want to ruin his fine clothing!" They stripped me of the red robe and my own outer garments until I was in just a loin cloth, then continued to beat me with sticks, kicks, and punches. Always their blows came when they were not in my direct line of sight; they abused me, and yet something in them still feared me. Red welts started to appear on my body. One of them punched at my nose, and blood started to flow from it; it would not be the last of my blood spilled this day. Buoyed by their brethren and their own braggadocio, they became more daring, and their blows became harder; one slapped me so hard across the cheek that I span and fell to the floor. Two of them yanked me back to my feet, pinioning my arms whilst they took it in turns to punch at my stomach.

They continued with their sport, seemingly taking it in turns to suggest different ways to strike and torture me, until, eventually, Pilate sent word that we were to rejoin him. They put my clothes back on me and half-heartedly wiped the dried blood from my face. The scarlet robe they did not put back on me – one of them had claimed that for his own.

DAY SIX: 08:00 – SENTENCED: BARABBAS OR JESUS

A large crowd had gathered outside Pilate's mansion: those who came to see how he would mark the festival (if he would mark the festival), the curious, those who had been urged to attend by the Pharisees and Sadducees, those who had been swept along in their wake. Pilate had spoken a few words to them earlier, placatory words – he wanted them on his side. I could hear the thrum of their conversation as I was brought into the room.

As was his way, Pilate thought to end his dilemma through manipulation and subterfuge. He consulted with his chief prison guard: "Tell me of some of the criminals we have below, their crimes." The guard whispered off a list of names, which I could not fully catch, until the last one. "Barabbas" I heard and "Insurrection… … Murder". Pilate nodded, said to the guard, "Bring him." When Barabbas was brought up, bewildered, blinking, wondering what fate awaited him (his expectation was humiliation and a painful death), Pilate went before the crowd again. He had Barabbas brought out to the left of the balcony; I was positioned to the right. Ivies were entwined around the balustrade of the balcony, their leaves dark and shiny; their shade only a little lighter than the wreath of laurel leaves that Pilate had placed on his own head – normally, these were the preserve of emperors. He revealed much of his own ambition in the wearing of them.

One of his vassals motioned for silence from the crowd. "Your Prefect, your Governor, the mighty Pontious Pilate would speak with you on this, your festival day." Pilate stepped to front and centre of the balcony. Loudly he addressed them: "I am aware that one of your traditions at this time of the year is that I mercifully release a prisoner, with full pardon. Whom shall I release? Jesus? Or Barabbas?" I know what answer he expected. But he didn't get it! Overwhelmingly, the crowd called out the name of Barabbas; scant few called my name and their voices were drowned out. I was not at all surprised by their response; it was predetermined. My accusers were, in reality, few, yet none would stand against them. But Pilate was clearly stunned; he took a step back as though struck. Clutching at the straw that they had misheard him, he asked again, "Who should I release? Should I release this man Jesus, or should I release the murderer, Barabbas?" I saw members of the Sanhedrin dotted throughout the crowd, ensuring that the name that was heard above any other was that of Barabbas. "And what should I do with this man?" he asked indicating me. "Crucify him!" yelled one of the Sanhedrin (although cautious to conceal that it was he who had shouted); others echoed his cry. More to himself than to the crowd, Pilate echoed words that I had said earlier, "Your will be done; it is not mine." He cleansed his hands before them and then stepped down. "See it is done," he instructed his chief prison guard.

The pressures of that which was to follow, combined with my earlier beatings, injuries and lack of sleep had taken their toll; my human frame let me down and I sank to the floor. At a signal, I was dragged to my feet and out. Now that the decision was made, it seemed that everyone was keen to get it over and done with, and not just for the sacred urgency expressed by the religious leaders. As I was dragged past Pilate, I caught his eye, saying to him, "One day soon, you will see me on clouds and at the right hand of the Father." I saw stark terror in his eyes before I was pulled away. I heard him say to one of his centurions: "Beat him, scourge him, then take him to Golgotha, the Place of the Skull, for I do not wish to hear his cries, his screams."

The crowd was starting to disperse, some heading straight for the crucifixion site, wishing for a prime space, others to find friends and families to share what had unfolded and probably thence to head also to that hill. I saw those of the Sanhedrin gathering back together, smug and smiling: they had got their way. Theirs was a crazy juxtaposition – wanting to be seen to be clean on the outside, by not entering the houses of those that they called gentiles and other such visible actions, so that they could gorge themselves on the Passover meal later, and yet inside, their betrayal left their souls mired in filth.

They led me now to an outer courtyard. In its centre stood a large wooden T-bar, its surface worn smooth by the bodies of those who had been tied to it previously to be given, variously and depending on the crime, six, nine, twelve, nineteen, twenty-nine and thirty-nine lashes, this last the maximum permitted. Once again, I was stripped of my outer clothes and then pinioned to the bar.

There seemed a long pause between my pinioning and the start of the punishment. Perhaps they were arguing over who should get the privilege of the task. And so, when the first blow came, I was not prepared in the slightest. The cruel, vicious whip snaked down and onto my back; I felt several of the cruel metal and flint pieces that are bound to the end of the strands of these things dig into my flesh, to be dragged across my back as the whip was withdrawn for the next lash. Involuntarily, I screamed aloud, in shock and in pain. How could one person inflict this agony upon another? How could they do so with apparent relish, taking pride in the hurt administered? The second blow fell, this time lower, across the small of my back but with the same tearing of my flesh. I grunted as the breath was forced from me, but I would not scream again. The third lash was much lower, across my calves; he clearly wished to inflict pain across every part of my body. He continued to follow that pattern, moving the blows up and down my body, tearing my flesh in myriad places. Twice or thrice he even whipped at my head. This was no accident – his blows were precise. He was well experienced at delivering them. No, it was intentional. One of the cords caught my ear, tearing away a part of the lobe; another snaked around and caught my eye. I was fortunate (if that is the right word) that it was the flat of the flint that caught my eye, so it bruised and puffed up but the sclera was not lacerated. Sometimes the blows came in quick succession, and sometimes there was a lengthy pause between blows, as he sought to maximise the torture through lack of rhythm, therefore allowing me no anticipation of when a blow might fall.

In all he delivered, with fearsome accuracy, forty lashes: one more than the maximum permitted. He might have continued had a voice not rung out, commanding: "Cease!" A silence fell on the yard. My flesh, a crazed archipelago of raw flesh and lacerations, oozed blood which trickled and dripped to the ground. Two guards – Roman soldiers now replaced the temple guards in taking the lead, although the temple guards remained on hand – came and untied me from the post. Without the ropes to support me, I slithered down the wood to the ground, too weak to rise. "Could you not even save yourself from this!" one of them hissed at me, in mocking contempt.

I was lifted to my feet but could not stand unsupported; my vision was blurred, watery; my head spun. Three of the temple guards approached me now, the first spoke, mockingly: "We must dress the mighty king for his coronation!" They put another robe on me; this time it was a purple one. Another had fashioned a crown of thorns from a nearby bush; he crammed it down on my head, the thorns gouged into my flesh, releasing further rivulets of blood. They surrounded me, laughing scornfully and jeering.

After they had taken turns at verbally abusing me, they brought out a heavy spar of wood and, having removed the purple robe but leaving the crown of thorns in place, placed it across my shoulders; once more, my arms were lashed and pinioned, this time to this cross bar, which stretched a cubit beyond my hands each side. Its weight and my weakened state toppled me backwards as they withdrew their support. I fell to the ground, unable to move. Sand covered the floor of the courtyard, and now that sand ground into my wounds, causing further agonies as it abraded my flesh.

The legionaries signalled to the temple guards. "Lift him; help him." They were reluctant to come near me, and not just because my blood would make them unclean. But they could see no alternative, so one took the end of the spar either side, seeking to avoid being near my arms, and lifted me to my feet using that. They led me out into the streets. As though the skies could no longer hold back the grief of witnessing my suffering, thunder rumbled, lightening flashed, and heavy rains started to fall again.

DAY SIX: FURTHER BEGINNINGS OF THE NEW BEGINNING

08:30 – Led to Calvary

After the weeks of drought and sunshine, the storms and beating rain, mixing with the rains that had fallen during the night, churned up the dry ground, turning everything to a quagmire. Despite the temple guards at the end of the spar, several times I slipped and stumbled. The first time, I fell fully to the ground; on subsequent occasions they were more prepared, and the guards yanked me upright using the spar. We had not gone far through the streets when one of the temple guards plucked from the crowds a man standing alone watching the procession pass by. He was a visitor to the city; he did not know what he was witnessing. The guard told him, "It is not seemly for us to be seen helping him; you must support him." And so, Simon the Cyrene came to my side, too afraid to say no and risk punishment; he put my right arm across his shoulders, his left arm across my back to support the left somewhat (the presence of that arm probably hurt, but I was in so many agonies that I hardly noticed it) and so together we carried my cross. Even with his help, I was too weak and kept stumbling, but he did not allow me to fall again.

The last quarter league added the extra challenge of inclining upwards as we headed for the plateau at the top of the mound called Golgotha, in the area of

Calvary. Rills of water ran over our toes, as though the rain waters had no desire to be present on that hilltop and witness that which was about to occur.

When we arrived at the summit, the Cyrene was relieved of his burden, and I was pushed to the ground. My spar, with me attached, was laid across a longer spar; the recesses in each were aligned to form a cross-lap joint. The end of this new spar, above my head, was propped onto rock to allow access to the joint; the two spars were knotted together, with my head being yanked this way and that as the rope was passed around it.

Whilst they had already lashed my forearms cruelly, tightly, to the cross spar, one of the stockier legionaries still applied his full weight to my arm, pinioning the limb further, in anticipation of the driving in of the nails. The rough wood of the cross pressed, agonisingly, into my whip-scarred back. I felt the sharp prick as the point of the iron nail was positioned at the base of my palm, adjacent to the fleshy end to my thumb. Involuntarily, I tensed, and then came the first hammer blow. The nail slid easily into my flesh, although slid is probably not the right word: with the roughness of the iron, it was more akin to the flagellation of my body now becoming internalised. Another strike and the nail slid further in, driving aside the smaller bones of my wrist, parting them, tearing sinews; it entered the gap between the radius and the ulna, to emerge from the flesh on the other side. In a distant corner of my mind, the carpenter in me approved of the oblique angle with which they were driving the spike into me: it would give extra grip in pinioning me to the spar; less danger of sliding off the nail. Now the point had emerged the other side of my flesh and met the first real point of resistance as it started to drive into the wood. The soldier swung the mallet with more force; this decreased his accuracy. Twice he missed the nail, and the hammer slammed into my fingers. The pain of the nail in my flesh was intense; the pain of that to which it portended was even greater. Those pains meant that the blows to my fingers hardly registered.

My ankles were crossed and tied together, but they were not tied to the spar. A longer nail was brought out and driven through both ankle joints and into the wood. There was no platform below my feet, when I was raised, my full weight would be on my arms, and that nail driven through my ankles.

09:00 – Crucified

Below my feet, the upright spar extended another five cubits, at its tip a large hole had been bored into the earth; the hole was rapidly filling with rainwater. To my left and to my right, similar activity was underway as two others were pinioned to wood; one of them bore the ministrations quietly, the other was screaming loudly. For a while, the rains ceased again.

The hammering had ceased now. A deathly silence fell; the screaming had stopped. At a signal from the centurion who was overseeing the process, the three crosses were pushed slightly forward; the three bases met thick board that protruded from the far side of those holes in the ground, halting further forward progress. Around the end of each cross spar, ropes had been wound; the ends of those ropes were held by two soldiers on either side and to the front, four in all for each cross. Those soldiers now took the strain on those ropes and started to pull; two other soldiers stood behind me, one either side of the top of the upright spar; they started to lift that end upward. Between them, the four pullers and the two pushers, slowly the cross arose until it was virtually upright. At that point, the base of the cross slipped jarringly into the hole; it thudded into place, jolting the three of us who were being crucified. Involuntary cries escaped from all three of us. I felt my weight pulling at the nails that had been driven through my palms and lower arms; they remained secure but pulled against flesh and sinew. I tried to reposition my weight slightly using my legs. That was a mistake: searing, tearing agonies assaulted me from the nail through my ankle. The ropes cut into my arms. There would be no position in which I might seek comfort for the hours ahead.

Further wooden wedges were driven in around the base of the cross, immobilising it in its hole. The noisier one, on my left, was swearing at the guards, haranguing them. I think he sought to drive them into spearing him to death, to find relief from the agony. He did not succeed. I felt further sinews straining, tearing in places; seemingly as easily as I had torn the bread this last night. Even breathing was hard: inhaling meant that I had to try to lift my body slightly; exhaling was easier, as my weight sinking back down forced the air from my lungs. Every breath caused pain, without respite; any tiny movement sparked renewed agony at my wrists and ankles and along my arms and legs as the pain spread through the muscles and sinews. My scourged flesh added further agonies as it dragged against the wood; blood dripped and seeped from these wounds, as it did, slightly more so, from my wrists and ankles. I tried to pray, but could get only as far as the word *Father* before the anguish and the agonies drove any further words from my mind.

And so, there I hung upon my tree, my life slowly, painfully, agonisingly, slipping away from me. A tree had started your downfall, and now here I was upon this tree, seeking to reverse that downfall.

He who I will not name came to tempt me again. At first, through the pain I did not know him. Subtly he whispered in my ear, "Mask the pain; it is within your gift!" I came so near to listening; the pain was indeed unbearable. But I could not cheat you all. To mask the pain would have been to blemish myself, to create a defect, then all would have been in vain. "Father!" I cried aloud. For a few moments, human frailty took me, and I passed from consciousness, only to reawaken moments later in fresh agony. I cried out again, "Father, Father, why have you forsaken me?" I could not feel His presence. "Yes, yes," came the insidious voice again, "He has abandoned you. You must look to your own salvation; just will it and you can step from this prison; you can trample those who have pinioned you; you can show your might, your glory!" With a supreme effort, I exorcised that voice, but I knew that it would return.

10:00 – My Clothes Divided by Lots

At the foot of my cross, the six legionaries who had pinioned me and raised the cross sat in a circular huddle. In their centre was a small pile of my clothes, including my own tunic, both the scarlet and purple robes and my sandals (the scarlet robe had been taken back from he who had tried to take it earlier; this dividing of clothes was the sole privilege of those who undertook the grisly tasks). They sought to use cleromancy to decide how the pile might be divided between them; the sandals were well worn and of little value, but they all coveted the robes and the tunic. They had flat bone discs; on one side of the disc were various markings, and the other side was unadorned. It seemed that to cast these particular lots they were tossed upward and then when they came to rest on the ground, the more marked sides that were visible, the higher the score. Each made three casts and totted up the scores; the winner of the round then removed one item from the pile (the pair of sandals, of course, counted as one item) as their prize until all the items were gone.

With their "prizes" safely stowed in their packs, they sat below my cross and now passed a skin of wine around the group, taking long swigs from it. Occasionally, one of them would glance up at me, but they paid me very little heed at all. Well, I suppose I was not going to go anywhere; they were probably more about keeping back any of the crowd who might stray too near to the crosses to aid the three of us victims in some way.

10:30 – Insults

A fair-sized crowd thronged around the crucifixion site: the curious, the onlookers, the hangers-on, the epicaricacists; some of the disciples were there too, dotted amongst the crowd, although by no means all of them.

More painful, still, than my whip-scarred back and the agony of crucifixion were those who last week counted themselves as my followers but who this week, twisted by the words, half-truths and downright lies of the Sanhedrin fed to them by the Pharisees and Sadducees, now stood shouting cruel jibes at me: “It’s true: if he really was the Messiah, he would save himself.” “How did he take us in?” “Why doesn’t he work a miracle for himself and just step down from that cross?” “They say he healed others. I never saw it myself, mind you; so, why doesn’t he heal himself of this?” “He cannot be the Son of God; God would not let him suffer in this way!” “Blasphemer!” “He’s no Son of David; more son of a donkey!” Some were silent, sympathetic, but they did not speak up.

Such is the power of the mob, and for some the weakness of the human mind, that they find it easier to follow the words of others than to think for themselves. If they were but to listen to their heart for the briefest of moments, they would hear the lies inherent within those words.

Briefly, I saw Barabbas in the crowd. He looked confused, still wondering how he was down there and I was up here. Though they have not been recorded anywhere (in part as he changed his name), he did great deeds ever after that.

11:00 – Harangued From My Left; Venerated From My Right

As though they represented the two sides of humanity, the two who hung one either side of me spoke to me through their pain. "Come," said the first, speaking with Satan's tongue, "if you are truly the Messiah, take us down from this place and free us! Help us to escape this pain and suffering!"

The second was quieter, though his voice still carried: "Quiet down! Do you not see it? You and I, we deserve this; it is the penalty that we must pay for our crimes. But he, he has done no wrong. I had heard that he came here to save us (though I ignored it), but now I understand his message and his calling!" He addressed me now: "Bless you, Lord, for this that you do for us this day. Remember me! Forgive me!"

That repentance, more than any of the other temptations, almost caused my resolve to break. But the end was nearly upon us now – an end that would bring new beginnings; the time had come. I turned my head slightly to the right, towards him. "Truly, I say to you, this day you will join me in Paradise!" I saw in his eyes that he believed that, though he spoke no more.

Like some echo rattling around a canyon, the sentiments uttered by those two came to me now in fragments from different parts of the crowd: "Save yourself, if you are who you say you are!" This mostly from the religious leaders and the Roman legionaries (although not all of these spoke this way). "Save us! Forgive us!" From my friends, family, and those who remained true. My human body was close to failing me now, to give up at last. "Forgive them all!" I managed; though my voice did not carry far in this world, it echoed awesomely around Heaven.

Now I knew that, had it remained with me, for all that I would have suppressed my Spirit, for all that I would have let my human side take the ascendancy, for all that I would have allowed the pains and agonies to suffuse me, the Spirit would have cushioned me. But with the Spirit withdrawn from me (in my pain and in my panic, I had started to imagine that it had fled, though not from fear), at that moment, I was completely, fully human. Then I truly knew great fear. And the pain became greater too, more real. This would be the death of me. Real death: a death that I would feel and experience firsthand. "Father, why have you forsaken me?" tumbled from my lips, for at that moment, I thought that it was so.

Of course, I had always known that this was necessary, but now that the moment came, I was filled with human fears, with human pain, with human agony.

Of a sudden, the evil one realised his error. He had not driven me to my death, he had driven me to my rebirth. He raced now, with one final roll of the dice, one final temptation, as he said, "You have proved yourself worthy of all praise, come now with me that I might set up your throne upon the mountain top, that you might judge the world, that you might punish those who have acted against you!"

12:00 – Darkness Descends

Such was my pain that my Father could no longer look on. Later, I was to learn that he felt my pain, magnified – he suffered even more greatly than I did, mental anguish can and does indeed cut deeper than physical pain – and that he could not bear to look. For the one and only time, he turned his eyes away from his creation. As his gaze left, the sky went dark. The world turned black. Night, it seemed, replaced day. Thunder rumbled in, mingling with the enemy's curses. The skies wept.

And there was no light.

And so, I became completely and utterly human; no longer a part of the Trinity. That was how it had to be. I had to die as a human for the prophecy to be fulfilled. I had to truly die to be raised from the dead. Nothing could be left. No Spirit (at that point, I still had my human spirit, which was an image, a reflection, of the Holy Spirit – just as yours is), no breath, for sure no heartbeat. All of it had to leave me; my Spirit left first, my heart stopped, my final breath seeped from my lungs: a silent whisper.

15:00 – Death

As I took my final breaths, many things I saw in my mind's eye: I saw the tears on my mother's cheeks, I saw Peter resolute once more, and I saw the veil of the Temple torn asunder (In another 45 years the whole Temple would be torn down, the Romans fulfilling that which we had determined). That tearing asunder symbolised its opening, making it accessible to all, changing its status from *private members club* to *no membership required.* As those last breaths left me, so too did my disciples. Some had already fled, now the rest fled too. They had heard the things that I had said, of that which was to happen, but they had interpreted them wrongly. Perhaps they had hoped that I would step from the cross. Or cheat death in some other way, to rise in a blaze of glory. Even though I had named the third day, it had not properly registered with them. They gathered now some way off, lost and truly afraid like small children, fearful of a dark and stormy night.

Death was the last and final of my new experiences; as with the other things that I have described – the sunrise, the oceans, the human touch – I experienced what death was truly like. I had thought of it previously as simply nothingness. And in a way it was. It was like the shutting of a nighttime curtain. But it was so much more so. My eyes stopped seeing; my ears stopped hearing; my lungs stopped drawing in the breath of life; the water of life I tasted no more upon my tongue; I felt nothing, neither physical nor spiritual; finally, I smelled no more, all aroma was gone, and that was, perhaps, the deepest loss of all. Nothingness took me. And I had no measure of how long I was nothing. From the moment when I was gone, to the moment of my return, nothing; like the gaps between the stars, but without the stars for comfort.

How easy it would have been to step from the cross, to end the pain, to hover above them, resplendent, mighty, fully awesome; they would have thrown themselves at my feet, fearful, terrified, subdued. But I knew, tempting though it was, that that would simply return them – you – to an atavistic state. My purpose was to take you on the next step of the journey, of your evolution, of your return to the Garden. To correct the deviation caused in that Garden, the Garden of Eden. To create in you a truer reflection of our image. That doesn't mean that we have two arms, two legs, a beard, brown eyes, so that's what you should aspire to. It was the image that we manifested in love, in compassion, in caring for you (so that you would care for each other).

A spear pierced the side of my already dead corpse: the guards doing their duty and ensuring that I was fully dead. Blood and water gushed forth. Seeing that spear thrust, an old man who had been in the crowd broke off and hurried back towards Jerusalem. That man was Joseph of Arimathea.

DAY SIX: BURIAL

Joseph of Arimathea sought an audience with Pilate. He had brought Nicodemus with him; he had not told those in the Sanhedrin of his purpose. Joseph and Nicodemus were both old now, old enough not to care what the Sanhedrin thought, free enough of their clutches to be able to think for themselves. They also took with them the centurion Longinus, who had overseen that day's crucifixions, he who had pierced my side with his spear.

They pleaded with Pilate for the release of my body so that they might bury it in the right and proper manner. At first, Pilate was reluctant;, he wanted me cast into the open pit like the others. But Pilate was worn down by the events of the day. He had heard about the sign at the Temple. He was fed up hearing my name; he just wanted a little peace. He quizzed the centurion for confirmation that I was truly dead and heard about the blood and water that had flowed, freely, from my wound. In the end he allowed it. But gave the centurion strict instructions to oversee the process and not to let my body out of his sight until it was in the tomb.

When they found out what Pilate had allowed (little remained secret in Jerusalem – all sides had spies), the Sanhedrin were furious. They too went to Pilate to demand he mount a guard at my tomb. "They will try to steal the body," they told him. "They will claim that he rose from the dead!" they asserted. "His body might cause more trouble than when he was alive!" they informed him. Pilate was incensed to have his word questioned, and yet he recognised the truth behind their sentiments. Angrily, he dispatched a small contingent of eight guards with instructions to find where I was buried and to ensure that the site was not disturbed.

It was by now twilight. The rains had ceased and somehow the moon that had the night before been but a crescent was full; it was as though time had been reset. Back at Golgotha, the centurion detailed a number from his legion to remove the wedges and lower the cross to the ground. They used pincers and a lot of sweat and effort to remove the three nails from my hands and feet. Of course, I felt nothing. I report this simply as events that occurred; at that moment in time, I was not aware of anything. I learned it only once my body and spirit were reunited.

Longinus signed that the body might be removed from the cross. It was Nicodemus and Joseph themselves who lifted me from the cross. They gently laid me on a board that they had brought with them. They removed the crown of thorns from my head and tossed it far from them, as though it was diseased. Starting at my feet, tenderly, reverentially, with great care, they wrapped me in strips of clean white linen.

As he watched the process, Longinus had a revelation. Tears flowed from his eyes, wetting his clean-shaven cheeks; he knew me for who I was, without doubt. From that moment, his life changed dramatically, but that is a story for another time.

Around my hands and feet, and particularly from my side, blood still seeped. It stained the fresh white linen, creating a mottled archipelago on the surface. The two men wound further layers of linen around these places. Now, only my head remained unbound. Joseph took out a comb and combed out my hair, which had become twisted and matted from all that had happened that day. When he was satisfied that it was as neat as he could make it, they wrapped my head too.

The board had two poles running its full length and beyond. Joseph and Nicodemus bent to take these poles and lift me. "Wait!" cried the centurion. "That is not seemly! My men will bear this load; you will lead us, and I will follow behind."

And so it was. Nicodemus and Joseph to the front, Longinus to the rear, and four legionaries carrying the board. They descended the hill and took the winding path that led to the nearby tombs. It was around a thirty-minute walk, as the tombs were built to be completely out of sight of Golgotha, the place of death. Many years since, Joseph had purchased one of these tombs for his own use, but he now gave it up for me. When we arrived there Nicodemus and Joseph asked to be the ones to take me inside the tomb, which was granted. They laid the board on a raised dais inside the tomb, removed the two poles and stood them against one of the walls. They spoke words of prayer over me; they commended my spirit to Yahweh, they prayed for forgiveness for those who had done these things to me; they said words of lament and mourning; they gave thanks for my life; they spoke from the psalms: they recited the thirty-seventh psalm; they included a fragment of the fifty-sixth psalm (verses three and four); they finished with psalm twenty-three: "The Lord is our shepherd; we shall want for nothing. In green pastures he maketh us lie to take rest; he leadeth us beside the calm, still, waters. He restoreth our souls! He guides each of us on paths of righteousness for His own name's sake. Verily! Though we pass through the very valley that is overshadowed by death, we will fear not the evil one: for Thou art with us; for Thy rod and Thy staff they bring us comfort. Thou preparest a bounteous table before us, even in the presence of our enemies: thou anointest our heads with fine oil; our cups runneth over. For, surely, Thy goodness and Thy mercy shall follow us all the days of our lives: and in the last days we will dwell in the house of the Lord for ever." Outside, Longinus listened intently. "Certe hic iacet Filius Dei!" he whispered to no one in particular.

At that moment, the second group of legionaries came stomping up to the tomb; a scattering of the

Sanhedrin followed in their wake. Longinus looked angrily upon them. Their bluster faded somewhat; they came with Pilate's sanction, but Longinus outranked even the most senior amongst them. And so it was one of the Sanhedrin who spoke: "Pilate has sent these men to ensure that the tomb is properly sealed, with the body secure inside. They are to guard it through the night too." Joseph and Nicodemus emerged into the moonlight. One of the legionaries entered with a torch to verify that the body was within; he emerged and nodded to his captain. To the right of the entrance, a large stone was leaned against the outer wall, ready to seal the doorway. A number of this second party attempted to shift the stone into place but could not move it. Some of Longinus's men moved to help them, but he waved them back. And so it was that some of the Sanhedrin themselves had to dirty their clothes, and their flesh, to help with the shifting of the stone. When it was finally in place, they inserted wedges, mortaring these, and the entire gap between stone and rockface. The Sanhedrin nodded their satisfaction; there would be no shifting that stone! Eight legionaries remained to guard the tomb: two posted on each side of the entrance, the other four at the points of the compass a little way off to ensure that none might approach unmarked. Joseph of Arimathea, Nicodemus, Longinus and his legionaries, together with the Sanhedrin (although they walked separately) returned to Jerusalem. It was now just before midnight.

DAY SEVEN: INTERRED

And on the seventh day, my empty body rested in my tomb.

DAY ZERO: HOME AGAIN

Day Zero, when the clocks were reset.

And on that third day, I returned from nothingness. At first, in the Spirit, I stepped across and into my Father's House; I went to stand once more at my Father's side. That return journey is very hard to put into clear words, words that will mean something to you. It was both long and at the same time instantaneous. I was refreshed as after a long and uninterrupted night's sleep; my mind was alert, my senses were sharpened. And there was my Father. We embraced. A single tear rolled down his cheek. "In you I am well pleased," he said. We broke our fast together and talked quietly, mostly of minor occurrences from my years on Earth. He knew, of course, all the big stuff.

I know from the imagery that we have left you that you picture my Father sitting upon a grand throne, with my own throne set slightly forward and to the right of that. That is indeed the best description that we can give in words that you would know. How we long for the day when the reality will be revealed to you and new words learned (and, certainly, old words forgotten) and you will walk the pastures of the New Jerusalem. Those pastures will cover the whole globe; the seas will be no more, there will be rivers and streams, but the last of the chaos waters – that were there from the beginning – will be gone. Subterranean springs will burst forth and water the land, as they did once before, in the beginning, before my Father created the first rains.

However, before I knew it, it was time for my other return, albeit for only a brief time. It was time for my Spirit to be reunited with my body, and for that body to be reborn as my Resurrection Body. The Resurrection Body needs no sleep; it does not know tiredness or exhaustion; it feels no pain, no hurt (inside or out); it does not age – it is simultaneously a teenage body and an octogenarian body, with all the advantages of both and none of the disadvantages of either. This time, the rebirth was not as a single cell; I was complete.

DAY ZERO: RESSURECTION

And there I was, back in my tomb but in a new body, my Resurrection Body; the old body was gone. Several of the angels had returned with me, rejoicing over that which was about to unfurl; their golden and silver light illuminated the tomb and the stone plinth on which I had been lain. I folded, neatly, my burial cloths; I would have no more need of the robes of interment. Three of the angels rolled the stone that had been placed across the entrance to the left. No light came flooding in: there were still several hours until dawn. For a while, I sat outside in the cool still of the early morning air. The angels departed on missions of their own. The legionaries who had remained resolutely outside my tomb all the previous night had found a quiet corner in which to sleep.

Some while later, he who tended to the gardens around these tombs arrived. Paying me no heed at all, he started his work of maintaining the plants that were in profusion around the area; some grew there naturally, some he had planted with his own brown, weather-stained hands. The paths too, he swept, even though he knew that by the day's end the dirt (mud now, rather than the dust, which had been much easier to sweep away) would have returned. It was important to him that the days started with everything presented as neatly as possible.

Presently, I heard soft voices approaching; another, angelic, voice cut across them: "He whom you seek is not where you expect to find him!" Their softly spoken words did not pause; perhaps they did not hear him. Five women turned the corner, heading towards my tomb; there were the three Marys (one of whom was my mother), with them came Joanna and Salome (my sister). Between them they were carrying jars of oils and spices, intending to anoint my body. I watched their approach; a smile of amusement passed across my lips. They were oblivious, also, to me, sitting there – to be fair to them, it was not simply that they were in rapt conversation, only the tiniest glimmerings of first light were peeping over the horizon.

I echoed the words of the angel: “He whom you seek is not within!”

They looked at me, suddenly aware of my presence; then they gasped, noticing that the stone had been rolled away from the tomb’s entrance. Ignoring me, they suddenly ran the final few yards, ducking into the tomb. I heard their cries of alarm. I heard a jar smash as one of them dropped it to the floor; the sweet smell of spiced nard emerged through the tomb door, mingling with the fragrance of jasmine which grew abundantly throughout the gardens. They stumbled back out, confusion and fear both seeking to take control of their features. “Who has done this?” one of them asked me. “Do you not know? Do you not know me?” They were not really listening to me (I laughed inside: those who have ears were still not always hearing!). I looked into the eyes of Mary of Magdala, “Mary, do even you not know me?" Suddenly, recognition came, and she fell to the ground, prostrate before me; she uttered one word: "Lord!" And that word loosed the blindfold that had seemed to cover the eyes of the others. Several repeated the word uttered by Mary; one of them said, "My son!" in a voice choked with tears. "Yes, it is me," I assured them. "It is as I said it would be; three days have passed!"

Overjoyed, they raced off in a confused babble of voices; they went to find one or two of my disciples to alert them to this turn of events. Not one of them remained with me. As they had approached the tomb, the women had been fearful and afraid, not the least in wondering how they might move the stone that sealed the entrance. Now, that fear had turned to joy!

I was alone in that garden once more.

There was a difference – and an important one – between my resurrected body and that of my friend Lazarus and the others whom I (and indeed, you) had, or will, raise. They have simply been called back to life; in their time, they are to die again. But the resurrected body is eternal, it will last forever; so far, only I have been given that reward.

I called Lazarus back to life. I did not resurrect him; the breath of life had entered him once more, but he had returned to his old body. My own resurrection was possible only because I am of Paradise; resurrection for Lazarus, and for all others, can only occur when Heaven comes down. That time is not yet; it is near (I think, but only the Father knows), but it is not yet. The day when you will all be clothed thus is still to come. Mine would be the first resurrection, the proof of that future, but no other would receive theirs until the day when all are raised. That one glorious day.

Some of the disciples returned and saw me on that day too; they did not know me at first either. In the coming days, I would visit all of my disciples, sometimes individually, sometimes in groups. I also made myself known to many of my wider group of followers and disciples as they met, as they journeyed, as they worked.

My message to all of them was the same: "Await me in that same upper room; assemble there; I will come to you there in the Spirit."

THE NEW JERUSALEM

My Father had been busy creating the New Jerusalem. It was not yet complete. But I got to be the first man to walk amongst its walls and dwellings, although that was a misnomer: there were no walls, and the dwellings are probably not as you would imagine them.

It is a strange thing, the Resurrection Body. It is both alike and yet not alike the human body: it was in many ways like learning to walk again. It was another very new experience for me, living in that Resurrection Body. It was in just about every way the same as my human body, but there were just a few subtle differences; those differences are mostly internal, hidden, delicate. Perhaps that is why it is so hard to get used to. It made it hard to be in one place; actually, that's not quite right, as it would be closer to the truth to say that I was in several places at the same time. It is equally hard to express the why of this. In part it was rooted in my Resurrection Body; in part, as Heaven has not yet fully come down.

I found it very hard to maintain a firm footing; clothed as I was in that body, but with Heaven not yet come down, it was near, but not quite near enough. One minute I would be walking alongside someone, or sitting at the table, just like I was that time with Cleopas, and then I would disappear from their sight. It was like trying to stand on the bottom of the ocean, with your body's tendency to float to the top – but quicker! Although, to be more accurate, this wasn't quite like bobbing upwards towards the surface; it was more like bobbing to the left or to the right!

During these last days I visited many. Some knew me not at all; some recognised me after a while; a scant few knew me at first sight. I shared news with them concerning that which would shortly come to pass; I gave instruction; I gave encouragement too – in the coming days, weeks, months, and years, their faith would be sorely tested. A test that every single one of them passed: not one of them denounced me; not one of them denied me.

Why did so many not recognise me upon my return? Even my own mother, and my own sister in that garden; surely it cannot have been the dim light alone? It is hard to pinpoint the reasons. In part it was that their eyes were somewhat clouded with doubt and a vestige of disbelief. For some, they feared to hope. In the greater part, though, it was probably that whilst I was reborn in my old body so too was it a new body, one that was fit for the New Jerusalem. I suppose the final factor at play was that throughout my entire time on Earth everyone saw me slightly differently anyway! Somehow, what they saw in me reflected their own ethnicity. Those with darker skins saw my skin as dark; those with lighter hair saw my hair as lighter; that same applied with my eyes too! So, perhaps, how they now conceived me was differently to those previous times? I suppose that it is a mystery that I could have solved, but I quite liked it as it was, so I left it so.

BACK TO THE BEGINNING

I had visited my disciples, individually and collectively, but they remained fragmented. I needed to draw them back together, to commission them for all that was to follow. For that, I needed a leader. And there was only one man for the job!

I had spent the night on the beach, praying to my Father. Whilst it was often better to pray from a mountain peak, this was simply due to the tranquillity of the place; it brings you closer to God. But I don't mean closer as in proximity; everywhere you are, you are close to the Father, as He is everywhere; He is not in some far-distant place looking down on us (and if He was, being up a mountain would not really bring you significantly closer!). No, it is the peace, the being one with nature, the being away from the city, that helps this. And so it was being on the beach that night: the gentle lapping of the waves the only sound. There was only the slightest of breezes, just enough to move the taller of the grasses that grew in clumps in the spaces between the sandiness of the beach and the earthiness of the land, but not enough to make a sound; it was silent like the flight of the owl. Indeed, flight was the main topic of our conversation, my Father's and mine, that night. How we needed the disciples to fly the nest and spread the Word, share the good news. Father had also told me of one that he had earmarked to join them in the near future, a most unlikely one! But, then, were all the disciples not unlikely ones? Once this next task of mine was completed, we agreed that I would meet him on a road and lead him, through blindness, into the light.

For a while, I had laid back on that beach and watched the stars in their slow dance across the skies. Now they were starting to wink out of sight as the thin light of pre-dawn crept into the sky. Time to gather! The first thing to gather was some pieces of driftwood for a fire. These were in plentiful supply, and I soon had a good pile of these stacked and ready. I also had a small pile of dried grasses and mosses to act as a base. I scooped out a shallow pit in the sand, putting a few smooth stones around its edges; in the centre, I put the grasses and the moss, with just a few flakes of driftwood around them. Then, it was the always tricky bit, striking a spark from a piece of flint enough to set the grasses and moss smouldering. After a number of strikes, I succeeded in making a big enough spark to catch some of the grass. I was rewarded with a few tiny flames and the thinnest plume of smoke arose from it. Gently, I blew on the grasses and the flames grew. Soon some of the flakes of driftwood had caught light, and I was able to place a few medium-sized pieces of wood over these in a tent-like shape. When these too were burning, I added the bigger pieces; I wanted them to charcoal down to give me some nice red coals to cook over.

Whilst the fire flared up and then settled down to a smoulder, I turned to my next bit of gathering: some fish. I walked a little way out onto the sea, carrying a small wicker basket. The water lapped gently around my legs; it was that joyful temperature when it is neither too warm, nor too cold, so I felt only its soothing presence as it splashed around my legs. I swept my basket through the waters and successfully scooped up five fishes, nothing too grand in size, but it would be sufficient. My guests would be bringing more – many more – with them. I returned to my now glowing coals and placed a smooth, flat stone over them. Whilst the stone was heating, I prepared the fish.

The arrival of a thin slice of orangey-red sun above the waters told me that it was time for my final gathering: the gathering of men. The growing light started to reveal a number of fishing boats out on the waters; it was one of these that I was particularly interested in. I saw the one that I was looking for not far out and quite close to the spot where I stood. I could see the occupants of the boat as shadowy outlines; there was not yet enough sunshine to reveal them fully. Out on that boat, there was much shrugging, frustration, and disillusionment: it was sitting high on the water, they had made no catch to weigh it down.

In an echo of three years past, I called out to them, "My friends, lower your nets on the other side!" They did as I asked, at that moment not from any belief, but more to do with proving to the stranger on the beach that they knew more about fishing than he did. Almost instantly, the nets were filled with fish, and the boat tipped precariously to one side as the weight of fish dragged it down. Instinctively, they let out the ropes linking the nets to the boat, not enough to let the fish escape but enough to stop the boat from tipping. Spray rose up as the boat's hull splashed down onto the surface. As though that spray had washed scales from their eyes, I heard one of them – Andrew – cry out, "It is the Lord!" At that shout, another of them – Simon-Peter – threw himself over the side of the boat and started swimming for the shore. He was crying out: "My Lord! My Lord!" Albeit amongst much spluttering, as he was swimming so vigorously that he kept splashing water into his own mouth. I called out to the others in the boat, "My friends, come ashore; let us break our fast together." They turned the boat towards me, and an opportune puff of wind took the sail and sent it scudding across the waters. It was not fast enough to catch Simon, but they arrived not far behind him. "My friends, bring some of your catch with you; my own catch is very small. It is now you who must feed with fish, and with bread!"

It was indeed a merry breakfast that we had on the beach that day. There were plenty of fish to go around, and they had also brought a basket of bread from the boat which their poor night's fishing had rendered them too depressed to eat. We ate together, and we sang songs, but I did not preach to them. Those days were past. I had told them all that I could, plainly and in parable.

They needed another guide now, one who would guide them, encourage them, and enhance their gifts. "My friends," I told them, "you must stay in Jerusalem for now and wait to be visited by our Spirit. It will prepare you and nourish you for that which is to come. Stay together for now. Strengthen each other. For soon, each of you must take your own path."

It was time to let Simon know that he was forgiven, to give him the confidence to be their leader once more, to draw them together as a group. I turned to him. "Simon-Peter, do you love me?" "Lord, you know that I love you above all others!" "Then tend my sheep." A few moments later, I asked again, "Simon-Peter, do you love me?" "My Lord, most assuredly I love you!" "Then, please, care for my sheep." He looked a little confused, why had I asked him the same question twice? Confusion turned to a spark of typical Simon-Peter anger when for a third time I asked him: "Simon-Peter, do you love me?" "Lord, how many times must I say it – you know all things; you know that I love you!" "Please, take great care of my flocks; keep them safely; see to their needs." He did not see it then, but as he thought on it in the hours that followed (in typical Simon-Peter fashion), the denarius dropped, and he realised that the three affirmatives that he had just made had wiped clean his previous three denials.

Suddenly, I was gone from them again. At first, they did not notice. I guess that they were getting used to this new way with me: unexpectedly there, and abruptly gone again! They continued excitedly talking amongst themselves. They felt great hope and had great expectations about the future now that they understood the reality of the resurrection.

On one of our last occasions together as a large group, we talked of the days to come. "How I long for those days, when the old will be swept aside," I told them. John turned to me, asking, "But Lord, why must these things be?" "Just as the farmer clears his field before he plants it anew, so must it be. The table must be cleared and cleaned before the banquet can be laid out. Many of you cleaned and mended your nets before you set out again. Remember Isaiah: 'he will swallow up death for ever.' We need many things to change. That is why I long for that time, John, when the words of Isaiah will be fulfilled; remember when he spoke of mavet and avelut? There will be no more need of crying, but my Father will still care; he himself will wipe away every tear. Death, mavet as we call it, will be lost from our vocabulary, neither will there be mourning! You will shout in glad tones, 'The prophesies are fulfilled!'

"That is when the third Jerusalem will come and the perfection that comes from three. In the first age, you lived in the first Jerusalem, then also called Eden. Though it might not seem it from the scrolls, that time was a passing long time. But then you fell. And that heralded the second age, the time of wilderness wandering. Jerusalem had become dust; you walked – walk – in it, though it is not known to you." I heard what they were about to say, so pre-empted it: "There is a place called Jerusalem, but it is but a shadow, an echo, of that which was and that which is to come. It must truly become dust before it can be remade. Just as man was made. The length of that age – which is this age – is not known to me; only my Father knows. But then, finally, will come the third and final age: the New Jerusalem. So, my fishers of men, clean your nets, mend them, in anticipation of that day to come!

"There will come a day when you will understand that which I am trying to express. It will be a day filled with joy for many! It grieves me greatly that on that day there will be some who will not receive their resurrection, will not have their bones reknitted together from the dust that they have become, will not have their sinews renewed, their flesh restored, will not receive the breath of life. I lament that some of those bones, through unrepented sin, will remain buried beneath the earth, that they will sink slowly, inexorably, further into the ground, growing closer and closer to the flames at the earth's fiery core.

Thus, my great hope is that, even if it is at the bitter end, there are those who will turn from their current paths, who will relent, who will seek forgiveness for their sins. For, even at the fifty-ninth second, of the eleventh hour, still there is hope. You might ask, *How can dust and bones repent, is that not impossible*? Well, please do remember that nothing is impossible with my Father! Remember too, that you are (fearfully and) wonderfully made in our image: just as we are three, so too are you three. You are flesh and bones, you have a soul, and you have the breath of life which animates the two. When the breath of life departs, then, at the moment of death, my Father is with each of you. Together, you weigh your life; it takes but a moment. It is the final opportunity for a last repentance. At that moment of death, not only does every eventful instant of your life appear to you, but so too the effects of those moments on others: the positive impacts and the negative ones. In that way, my Father opens your eyes and your heart fully and judges any true repentance – or any thanks – for those things.

Actually, I should say that it is almost the last, for so great is my Father's love for you that, as the flesh and bones go into the ground, the soul goes to another place. It is there that it may be read again, intentions revealed, and true repentance discovered."

On the last occasion that I sat with the eleven; we shared another final supper – this one really would be the last one for some while to come.

"Boys," I said, "you have seen much over the past few years. Maybe you had better write it all down!"

DEDICATIONS

I am, of course, indebted to the books which provided the framework for this one and, therefore, the writers of the four Gospels, without whom I would not even have got started.

I also have to thank Barbz, who led me to salvation; although probably neither of us knew that that would be the case. And, so too, to the Lighthouse Church, Portland, where it all happened.

To my extended family in the Vineyard Church, especially Wellingborough, which was grafted together with Raunds to become Nene Valley Vineyard and bore much fruit. There are too many family members to list individually, but it would only be right to mention the remarkable Senior Pastors Tom and Ashleigh Nicholson, and their delightful children, Elsie, Ada, and Eden.

My thanks to Tim and John, creators of The Bible Project, both of whom I have spent so many hours listening to, often on long drives. They were great company, but more importantly, they really helped my thinking, exploration, and depth of knowledge.

The fact that all the text to this point is so clean and error-free is thanks to the invaluable support of and niblets of wisdom from Melanie Cotton (the Gimlet-eyed Grammar Tickler®), who had the challenging task of detecting my errors typographical and otherwise.

To my mother, who first inspired my love of the written word, reading to me and then teaching me to do that for myself. I hope that I was equally inspiring to my precious children, Ian and Amy.

Finally, to the myriads of other books that I have read on the subject matter, far too many to mention here, although none of which are plagiarised herein but all of which have helped me to turn over mental, creative cogs.

ABOUT THE BOOK

In many ways, this book needs no introduction, being based as it is upon the most famous book in the world (sorry JK, JRR, but it is true!). But I thought I ought to set out one or two things concerning the text, and my purpose in writing it. I hope that what is written is written with all due reverence. There are parts of this book that are complete works of fiction. Actually, you might argue that much, or indeed all, of it is a work of fiction; I don't pretend for one moment that the contents are scholarly and based upon irrefutable, carefully researched, fact; the contents are based upon the true facts, as set out in The Bible, but are pure conjecture in their interpretation, in respect of the thoughts, feelings and emotions. What I meant by my initial 'works of fiction' statement is referring to the sections of the book where I have let my imagination run wild; for example, the scenes in Joseph's workshop.

There are many fine books written proving the history of that which occurred. There are an equal number of wonderfully researched tomes debunking many of the claims made against Christian beliefs. I do not believe that I have anything significant that I could add to those, so I wanted to take a different approach, exploring emotions and feelings, taking a descriptive angle. That is of course not something that can be researched; by its very nature it has to be speculative.

That approach also meant that I did not want to simply retell the story; so there may be places, dear reader, where I have missed out moments that you might count as essential, and included that which you might feel is inconsequential.

My intention in writing this book is to try to bring a new aspect to such well-known events; I do not presume to *know* the reality of the things that I describe. It is, perhaps, my version of a song of worship; as I do not have the necessary to create one of those. Or a bringing to life, as has been done many times, with great success in the world of film – most recently in *The Chosen* – but with words rather than celluloid. I sincerely hope that I have not over-presumed and descended into blasphemous territories; it is absolutely not my aim to shock or cause offence. My objective for this book is simply to offer an alternative viewpoint, to open up the thoughts of the reader. So, it is aimed at neither Christian, nor non-Christian, readers; it is here for anyone to enjoy. And I do indeed hope that you enjoy it! I am confident that there are enough buried 'Easter Eggs' to keep even the most learned of readers entertained!

The book is not written as a history; I have not spent long hours poring over dates and chronologies to reach a thread on which to hang the narrative. I felt that another rewriting of the history would, probably, bring nothing new. So, please, forgive all the 'inaccuracies' (some narratively intentional, some otherwise); just read it how it comes. I have intentionally allowed some biblical inaccuracies (and some theological ones) where I feel it helps the narrative. There are probably some unintentional inaccuracies, too! For those, I apologise.

Jesus was able to see the world through our (human) eyes; so now let us try to see the world through his!

You may disagree with some of my interpretations, assumptions or storylines. And that is great! I think that, for any author, in any genre, if their book prompts thought, then that is the greatest compliment of all! So do feel free to challenge away, it will give me great joy; I will take no offence!

My approach to the writing in offering it from a first-person perspective (this element is clearly one of fiction) is to personalise the story; to draw the reader in through the biographical approach; to help readers to imagine some of the harsh realities of that time; a world that was very different from our world of today (but one in which hopes, fears, emotions, doubts, and realities were much as they are now).

Bruce A J McLauchlan

Printed in Dunstable, United Kingdom

68098852R00188